Playing with Fire II

Whitney Cason

Whitney Cason

ISBN: 13-978-0-9991060-3-7

DEDICATION

Dedicated to everyone who kept pushing me to finish. For anyone who didn't let me quit. Thank you for reminding me that this is my passion, and you never quit on something you love.

Enjoy

INTRODUCTION

So, I'm sure you all have been wondering what has been going on with me. Well, to be honest, it hasn't been easy.

Trey and Liyah stayed together even after everything that happened. I thought for sure she was just going to be a rebound situation; and would be nothing more than his baby mama that he would have possibly regretted later. Well, all that changed when my mom told me they had gotten married. He barely waited for the ink to dry on the damn divorce papers. I'm sure Liyah had something to do with that, but I couldn't be certain. I knew at that moment he wasn't even thinking about me anymore. I guess whatever he had with Liyah was "real".

After our divorce was final and they got married, Trey and Liyah decided to move to Miami, where he had planned on opening a new restaurant as a part of his expansion plans. Liyah felt like it would be best for them to get out of Atlanta after she had the baby and start their new legacy in a new city. I also knew that she knew that Trey and I had always had plans to move to Miami as well, so I took that as just another shot at me to say she had what I always wanted with Trey. Little did she know, I had my own plans and had begun to get my own life together and it did not include worrying about the Wrights.

Liyah put out a restraining order on me shortly after the incident at Trey and I's house. How crazy is that? I guess she felt as if I was some sort of "threat" to her and Trey. Little did she know, I was less of a threat to Trey than I was to her. If she wasn't pregnant, I would have come back for her ass. I made a promise to myself that one day, we would sit down and finish this conversation. Hopefully, for her sake, I won't be a raging bitch ready to whoop her ass this time.

After a few weeks, I got a letter saying that the restraining order had been dropped. Trey later called and explained that he spoke with Liyah and agreed that since I was not causing any issues and they were not causing any issues, there was no point in having a restraining order in place. We also agreed that Trey and I would still need to have contact with one another for arranging visitation with Chelsea. I told him it was fine. I figured Liyah was doing the most, because she is known for being a drama queen. I thanked him for having the conversation with her at least, and that as long as she can remain civil, I can remain civil.

Deep down, I couldn't blame Liyah totally for all that has happened. It was easy, but it was not fair. I was the one who was doing the dirt in the marriage; and really Trey committed the worst betrayal. It was only after I cast the first stone, though. I let other men occupy my time, which caused me to miss out on what was important; which was Trey and Chelsea. I take full responsibility for messing up my marriage and my relationship with my daughter because now, all she sees is how Trey and I are just co-parenting and not being a happy family that I had always dreamed of us being.

When my mother found out, she was so disappointed in me. She couldn't speak to me for at least a week. I was pretty messed up about that, because it takes a lot for my mom to be upset about things, especially when it comes to me. When we talked, I felt like I was 16 and got caught sneaking my boyfriend in the house or stealing or something. Once we were done with that, I had time to really think and realize that I not only messed up my relationship with Trey, but also potentially damaged the image Chelsea had of me as her mother. I'll admit, I felt like shit but I'm glad my mom was able to have that real woman-to-woman talk with me. It helped me do some inner work with myself and really be a better woman and mother.

Tara slowly started to distance herself from me as well, which was to be expected. I could tell that she wanted to forgive me for what happened between Channing and I, but in the end, she decided that she was moving back home with her parents to have more support with Josh. We continued to talk every now and then, but then our conversations became few and far between. With the things I had done to the ones I love; I couldn't blame her for wanting nothing to do with me. I was surprised that she continued to talk to me as long as she did, but I always prepared myself for the day that we might lose touch. When she told me she was moving, she promised that we would still remain close and keep in touch, but soon enough, she began to move on with a new life and a new man, and I started to hear less and less from her.

With me losing the last good friend I had in Tara, and also losing my best friend and husband, I decided that maybe it was time for me to start a new chapter in my life as well. I took a few months, let Chelsea stay with my mom, and moved to DC to start establishing a new office and new life there. I set up a remote office there, so that I could still run CT Publishing in Georgia and in DC. Once I had all the paperwork set up and established, I began to look for a place for Chelsea and I to stay. I found a great realtor who was able to find a wonderful house in a great school district and a great neighborhood. It took several months of back and forth, a lot of remote interviewing for staff for the DC office; however, pretty soon I had a new fully staffed publishing office in DC, a new home and before we knew it, Chelsea and I were packed up and ready to begin a new chapter of our lives in a new city.

Things appeared to be going well. The adjustment from two-parent household to one-parent household was difficult, but I made it work as best I could. Things were going so well in DC, that I also found a few authors there to publish. Since my DC office was a remote office, the staff was smaller there; however, they were still an awesome team and I still had an agent who was able to find some very great writers who were ready to publish and had some great work. I had another two editors on staff and a marketer as well. And my executive assistant who kept the office running like a well-oiled machine whenever I had to go to Atlanta to check on things there. Despite my personal troubles, my work and my professional successes never seemed to waver, and especially being in a new city where no one knew much about Chante Wright, the cheater who screwed up a good thing and had the scandal of a lifetime. In DC, CT Publishing was still a successful thriving Black-owned publishing company; owned by an African American woman and set to be one of the greatest publishing companies on the East Coast.

In the divorce decree, Trey and I settled on having joint custody, and we split different holidays and school breaks so that Chelsea can have as much opportunity to visit with her father. I was able to retain sole physical custody, and Trey did not pitch a fit when I told him we were moving to DC. We both agreed that since we were both relocating, we would both meet in Atlanta so he could get Chelsea for his breaks and holidays. I usually stay for a few weeks to a month or so; check on things at the home office and spend time with my mom. We manage to stay very civil with each other, but I can see in Trey's eyes that he feels so betrayed by my actions. Every time I see him, I wish I could take it back, but I can't. Everything is still very fresh, and there are wounds that have not yet healed from what has happened. The only thing I can do is be a better person now, which I try to be every day, whether Trey truly forgives me or not.

Overall, I think things are as good as can be expected, based on how it all went down. These days, I'm just trying to raise my daughter, keep a peaceful relationship with my ex-husband and his new wife (it burns to even say that), and keep being a bomb ass writer and publisher. That should be easy enough, right?

Well, let's see just how easy it can be......

ONE

As the old saying goes, "there's no place like home," and even though I wasn't home, my mother's house was a close second. I turned the key and walked inside.

"Hello? Mama, where are you guys?" I called out through the house, which was completely dark. I usually tell her to keep a light on in this house because it gets so dark in here.

"Now, she told me they would be here when I got home, I wonder where they are?" I thought.

Just as I was looking around, I heard a door open and small steps running towards me down the hallway. I smiled wide as I knew exactly whose feet those were.

"MOMMY!! You're back!" Chelsea said as she barreled into me with her arms open wide to embrace me. I returned the gesture and picked her up and spun her around.

"Hey baby girl! How are you? Did you miss me?" I said. I was so happy to see my little girl I couldn't contain myself. It's something about seeing that smiling face after coming off a six-city tour that makes everything feel right in the world again.

I had just got back from being in Toronto, finishing up a tour from my recently published short story series that I co-wrote with another author who CT Publishing just recently added on. We also hosted some creative writing workshops and I hosted some book signings for previous work that I published as well. It was a great promotional opportunity for my newest book to be released at the end of the summer, which I had to start preparing for once I got back to DC. It was one of the best tours yet, and the fan base was growing constantly. It was the first time I was able to secure booking a stop in another country. I had secured her place in the literary world as a best-selling author, and it looked as if I would be labeled as one of the 'up and coming' in the urban genre of writing. I was ecstatic, and so was she. Every signing was a success, and we had launch parties and workshops that were packed houses. It was nothing short of a blessing after all I had been through in the past two years. Aside from all my personal drama, and moving, I had been a very busy writing bee.

I turned on the light and sat down with Chelsea. I showed her all the pictures I took in New York, Chicago, Toronto, Houston. She was amazed at all the buildings as I flipped through the pictures.

As I as showing Chelsea my pictures, I could hear my mother getting out of her chair in her bedroom and walking towards her door, "I figured that was you coming in my house without knocking."

"Yes, it was me, mama. But why are y'all in the back of the house? What if I was a burglar?"

"I'm sure we would have been ok. I do have a gun in my bedroom," She laughed.

I rolled my eyes and got up to give my mom a big hug. "How was everything?"

"It was great. Chelsea and I had tons of fun, right baby?" She said as she looked over at Chelsea.

"Yep!" She replied.

"Well that's great! I'm glad she wasn't much trouble. Thanks again for watching her this time. I know usually I take her with me, but this tour was a little longer than normal. I don't think she would have lasted."

"Yea, I know. This was six cities. The longest I've ever

been on. I'm getting to be pretty popular now mom."

"Oh, I'm not complaining, baby. I'm proud of you. I think it was just an adjustment for Chelsea is all. But she had fun hanging with her grandma, ain't that right, baby girl?"

Chelsea nodded as she continued to scroll through all my pictures.

"Well I appreciate it. Work is definitely picking up for me. I'm just getting back and I've got to get ready for the release of my book at the end of the summer. I'll be heading to LA for that book release as well. Your baby is heading to the big time, ma!"

"I see! I'm so proud of you, girl. You're doing so well."

I stayed with mom that night and hung out with Chelsea the entire night. I was so happy that our relationship improved in the last two years. When I was dealing with all my bullshit, my relationship with her definitely took a hit. I was so focused on running the streets and dealing with all the drama that Trey and I were going through, I wasn't there for her when she needed me. There was so much that happened that I could never forgive myself for. The things that happened between Trey, Liyah and I were things that I never wanted Chelsea to grow up and see me doing; things that I don't even want her to grow up and do as an adult. Every day I try to erase some of those bad things and do the right thing by her. My mom helps as well, and Chelsea seems to be opening up to me more.

After Chelsea went to sleep, I went into my mother's bedroom to see if she was awake.

"Ma, are you sleeping?" I called out to her.

"No, baby. I'm watching the news. Come in."

I crawled into bed with my mother like I was a toddler again and snuggled up right next to her. I always love coming to visit her because no matter what, I get a little spoiled.

"What time are you meeting Trey in the morning so he can get Chels?" my mother said as she continued to watch the TV.

"I texted him earlier and he said that he would meet me at eleven. He said him and Liyah are both coming," I said as I rolled my eyes.

"Still not getting any better?"

"Hell no mama. Matter of fact, it feels like it gets worse every time!"

"Well, maybe one day he won't bring her with him."

I chuckled a little, "I'm sure that won't happen, ma. If I don't know anything else, I know Liyah is going to watch him like a hawk, especially around me. Plus, she is going to have something new she is going to feel the need to throw in my face. She has no choice but to come and be messy at our drop off."

"Well, I'm going to pray on that, baby. Because she is a hot mess and then some. I can't believe that at one point you both were so close; like sisters even. Now it's just so bad."

"I know, mama, but it's partially my fault too, so sometimes I feel like I'm just dealing with my consequences."

"That doesn't give her the right to be a bitch though, Chante. That's my two cents and that's all I'm going to say about it."

We both continued to watch TV until we fell asleep. Once I woke up, I pulled the comforter up on my mom and left her to rest. I went into my room and pulled out my notebook to jot down some ideas I had been thinking about, and then eventually hit the sack. I had to get up early and prepare for yet another dramatic ordeal with Trey and Liyah Wright.

TWO

The arrangement with Trey had been a civil one; or as civil as one could be. The divorce was finalized about a year ago, and it was quite amicable; no matter how dirty and messy Liyah wanted it to be. She was in Trey's ear every step of the way trying to degrade me and berate me through the process. Although Trey hated me, he always told Liyah that she would respect me in his presence, "no matter what, she is the mother of my first-born child, so you will respect her, or we will have problems." That usually always shut her down. Even as cordial as he could be, he still has yet to forgive me. We rarely speak for more than five minutes on the phone. He usually only asks how I'm doing and if Chelsea needs anything, before he says he must go, and our conversation is dead. I can't say I don't blame him for not having much to say to me, but I would have hoped by now we could have a better conversation.

I texted him when I woke up the next morning to make sure we were still good for the time we agreed on so that he could pick up Chelsea for the remainder of the summer.

"Hey! Just checking to make sure 11 is still good for you. I'm getting Chels up now to get her ready."

"Um, this is Liyah. 11 should be fine. Just make sure you have everything ready because we plan to pick her up and head right back to Miami. Thanks."

I immediately rolled my eyes and let out a long sigh. *"I swear she does this shit on purpose."* I thought to myself. I told myself I should be 15 minutes late just to piss her off, but I decided against it. Trey doesn't deserve for me to be a bitch and it affect him as well. I threw my phone on the bed and proceeded to start getting Chelsea ready to see her dad.

After I got Chelsea ready, I went ahead and got myself together as well. I walked into the bathroom and began to run the water and prepare for a nice long shower. Dealing with Trey in this capacity is always so formal and awkward, and I wish it didn't have to be. There has been so much I wanted to say, but I know he wouldn't listen.

When the water was hot enough, I took off my old t-shirt that I slept in and got into the shower. I let the steaming hot water run down my body as I stretched. It felt amazing. I washed up, threw on some clothes and double-checked all of Chelsea's bag to make sure she had everything she would need. Once I was finished, we stood at the front door as my mother said her good-byes to Chelsea.

"You ready, baby girl?"

"Yes mommy!" Chelsea said with a wide grin on her face.

"Alright! Let's roll," I said as we kissed my mom good-bye and headed towards the car.

I loaded up the car on Sunday afternoon, preparing to meet Trey so that I could drop Chelsea off with him so that they could begin their summer vacation together. In the divorce, it said that one person had to drive one way to get her, but Trey and I decided to amend that and agree to meet in Atlanta. It gave us a reason to visit our parents and friends that were still there, and also the opportunity to manage our businesses where they originated. It also gave Chelsea a chance to see my mom and Trey's parents.

As I pulled up, I could see Trey's black Range Rover truck parked at Piedmont Park, our usual meeting spot. I pulled up right next to him. I looked over at him and gave him a polite smile. He looked over and waved. Chelsea and I both got out of the car, as did Trey. I noticed that Liyah was with him, not wanting to leave Trey's side for anything, as usual. As soon as she rounded the corner of the truck, her hand was intertwined with his. I wanted to roll my eyes until they fell out of my head, but I kept my composure.

"What's up, Chante?" Trey said.

"Nothing much Trey. How you been?"

"I can't complain much, everything is going well for us."

I could see Liyah out of the corner of my eye, continuing to smirk at me and roll her eyes. She finally decided to speak up.

"Yea, Trey has been doing really good! The restaurants are blowing up all over the state and we are constantly expanding; not to mention, Trey Jr. is growing up like a weed."

I rolled my eyes and tried to sound as supportive and cordial as possible, "well that's great Liyah! I'm glad you all are doing well. I see management is going well for you, congrats!"

"Thank you," she said, looking away. I could tell that trying to be polite is literally killing her, so I decided to focus my attention on Chelsea and her father.

Most times, our drop offs aren't usually this tense; however, whenever Liyah comes she has been known to want to show her ass most of the time.

Chelsea ran towards Trey, which naturally broke the tension. "Daddy!!" she squealed as she ran straight into his arms.

"Hey sweetie! How are you? I missed you so much." he said.

He grabbed her up and hugged her like he hadn't seen her in years. She doesn't visit with him as often during the school year, in order to not keep her out of school too much, but I allow him to FaceTime her every day when she's at home with me. Chelsea was just as excited to see Trey and it showed all over her face.

"Daddy, I have to tell you all about school and what happened! It was so much fun, and I got a ton of awards at the end of the year." She said with a beaming smile on her face.

"That's right. Unfortunately, I started my tour right before her awards ceremony, so I had to get my mom to go see it for me. She FaceTime'd me in, so I could at least see her accept all of them."

"Well, why didn't you call? I'm sure Trey and I could have flown up to see her. At least her *father* should have been the one there *in person*." Liyah said with major attitude. It took all the strength I had to bite my tongue in front of Chelsea, and Trey could sense it. He decided to stop her in her tracks.

"Liyah, calm down baby. It's ok. I'm not upset about it and you shouldn't be either."

"Yea, especially because she isn't your damn daughter." I thought to myself.

Liyah sucked her teeth and focused her attention on Chelsea.

"Well, Miss Chelsea. Are you ready for a fun-filled summer with me and TJ?"

Chelsea looked at Liyah and shook her head yes.

"Well, I guess it's time for you to go. Let me get a hug before you go," I reached out my arms to hug Chelsea. Chelsea shifted her weight from Trey's arms to mine, as I engulfed her in the biggest hug and kiss.

"You be good now, ok? Do what your daddy and Ms. Liyah say, ok?"

"Oh, she usually calls me mom when she's at my house,"

13

Liyah chimed in.

I shot a glare at Liyah that could kill. She continued to look at me, begging me to make a move on her. I wanted to punch her in her smart-ass mouth, but I was holding my child and she was the only reason I didn't. Little did I know, Trey caught wind of her expression and came to my rescue.

"Liyah, stop it! Here we are trying to act like civilized adults, and you are trying to cause drama. You will not do that in front of either of my children. I won't have that shit; do you hear me?" he said.

I stood and stared at Liyah, trying hard to contain my laughter at this point. Liyah looked up at him with puppy dog eyes and said, "I'm sorry baby."

"You need to direct that to Chante, not me."

Liyah mustered up as much kindness as she could towards me and said, "I'm sorry Chante; that was out of line."

"It's ok, Liyah. Let's just move on,"

I walked Chelsea over to the backseat of Trey's car and put her in. Trey went ahead and grabbed her bags out of my trunk.

"You be good, ok?" I said.

"Yes, mommy! Love you! See you soon!" she said. Chelsea gave me a kiss on the cheek and hopped in her seat and put on her seatbelt.

Trey put Chelsea's bags in his trunk. Since Liyah had already been embarrassed, she secluded back to her side of the truck and got inside. She continued to shoot daggers at me, even while she was in the truck. I didn't really pay her any attention. I wanted to speak to Trey about some things. As Chelsea was getting in the car, I motioned for Trey to come to the side. He walked over towards the sidewalk so I could talk to him.

Once Liyah was back in the car, Trey said, "I'm sorry about that. I know this is still crazy, but I have told her about that shit in front of Chelsea and...."

"You're fine, Trey. Really, I know it's not like you are condoning that behavior from her. I mean I really don't know why she continues to do that; I'm the one who lost in this situation, you know?" I said. I realized once I made that statement, it made things sort of awkward. We both sort of looked away from each other. I quickly decided to change the subject.

"Anyway, are you coming home for Christmas?" I asked.

"I'm not sure right now. You know the holidays are the busiest time for the restaurant down this way. Everyone is visiting the south and want to come there. So, I'm not sure what my schedule will look like."

"Well, I wanted to bring Chelsea down for Christmas break, plus I will have some events going on down in Atlanta, so it will be the perfect time for her to come down to see our parents. I also wanted to plan something special for Christmas, to get all the grandparents together to see her. I know you usually get her that entire time, but I was going to see if you were going to be here it wouldn't be so bad," I said.

"I'll try to work some things out, because I would love more time with her. I know your mom is into Christmas way more than my family, but you know we love to party," he said with a slight laughter. I laughed with him

"Well, ok. I just wanted to let you know. If you do decide to come up, let me know and we can set up something," I said.

"Ok, that's cool. Are you heading back to DC today?"

"I will probably leave out later tonight. I may spend the rest of the afternoon with my mom," I said.

"Cool. Well, let me get these ladies out of here and back to

South Beach. You know one day, you should bring Chelsea all the way, and come let us show you around."

"I'm not sure if your wife is ready for that, but if she is, let me know and I'll take a vacation," I said giggling.

We parted ways after that. Trey, Chelsea and Liyah drove off heading back to Florida, while I drove back to my mom's house. For the rest of the afternoon, I spent some quality time with my mother. We went out to lunch and then got pedicures at her favorite nail salon. After that, we went home, changed into some sweats and laid on the couch watching marathons of *Love and Hip Hop.* I had already made the decision to stay one more night, so I cooked dinner for her and we ate and talked about my eventful day with the new 'Wright's'.

"So, how was the drop off today?" my mother asked me.

"It went well, of course Liyah was there being a bitch as usual."

"Why does she have to come every time Trey gets Chelsea? Shouldn't she be running his restaurants or something'?"

I laughed, "Yes mom, she should. And it's only occasionally that she decides to come along. But I guess she is still scared I might steal Trey from her, so she needs to watch me around him."

"Well, I just don't like it. She has done enough already, messing up your family and all. It's such a big mess!" she exclaimed.

"Ma, you have to remember, I cheated on Trey. I made the mistakes. Yes, what Liyah did was foul, but Trey did it too. The only reason I have learned to forgive him is because we have a child together. And I can be civil with Liyah because I have to respect that that is his wife now."

My mother rolled her eyes and mumbled under her breath,

"It's still a damn mess. That's all I'm saying."

I laughed and continued to watch TV with her. Once she fell asleep, I went up to my room to start packing for my journey back home to DC.

THREE

When I returned home, I had no time to think about Trey because my work life was in full swing. I had another trip planned towards the end of the summer, and we had to have the right lineup. It would be my first time heading out to California, and I was beyond excited. I have received a lot of fan mail and feedback pleading with me to do more events out there, and once I finally made the announcement that I was holding a couple of signings and readings out there for my new book release, the fans went crazy.

With the release of my third novel, I had planned on having a few more events on the West coast, and my agent was even able to pull some strings and get me a live reading event scheduled to be held in London next year! Professionally, I was definitely having the best time of my life. At least no one could take *that* away from me.

I was sitting in front of my MacBook in my apartment in DC, speaking with my editors and public relations team back at my main office, as we began to go over all of the events we had scheduled for the West Coast and which authors were going to be featured along with me. I always try to bring my newest author on the rise, so that they can gain exposure and begin to build their fan base. I also had a list of authors from the company who had recently released books that would be accompanying me.

With Chelsea spending time with Trey, it gave me all the time in the world to plan and prepare. My team and I had also discussed my need for new headshots, since I hadn't really had any done in about two or three years, so I was telling them about how I had recently booked a photo shoot for a local magazine. They wanted to do a full interview on me and my publishing company and how the photographer was going to also do some headshots for me as well because she knew I was an author. It would be my first time getting this level of exposure here in DC. I was beginning to expand my name and my brand, so I knew that my company and my writing career was taking off to a new level. My team seemed to be thrilled with the vision I had in mind for myself here, and I had everything in place to get jump-started.

The next week, I had an entire glam squad at my office, getting me pampered and prepped for my photoshoot. The magazine had booked hair, makeup, wardrobe, and even had a pretty popular DC photographer to shoot me, Nia Maxwell. Nia Maxwell has done photos for different magazines across the DMV area, and just recently landed her gig with the DC Black Journal. She was also pretty big in the digital spaces and social media as well. She was definitely coming into her own in print magazines. This was a pretty big moment for the both of us. I heard someone mention this would be her debut spread, so I was flattered and honored to be a part of the process.

Shortly after I got my makeup done and was into my first outfit of the shoot, Nia came in and introduced herself.

"I finally get a chance to meet the infamous Chante Thomas!" she said as she extended her arms to hug me.

I returned the embrace, "Nice to meet you, Ms. Maxwell."

"Oh girl, you can call me Nia. We are about to have some fun today. I am so honored to shoot you, Ms Thomas," I was in love with her energy and positive attitude almost instantly.

"Well, in that case, you can just call me Chante. I'm not too big on formalities unless I'm in a big meeting. Today, I'm hoping to have a little fun with this shoot. I hope I look ok," I said. I had put on a little weight since I got to DC, but all it did was just make me look thicker and more attractive. I know the camera adds ten pounds but I'm hoping Nia is a master with this camera and can take them back if I need her to.

Nia quickly reassured me, "trust me Chante, you look AMAZING!" I love the wardrobe they picked out for you and your makeup is flawless! I can guarantee these pictures are going to come out looking perfect!"

"Thank you! I'm glad. I don't know if they told you, but I haven't had my headshots done in so long. And this is my first magazine shoot. I'm a little nervous, but hopefully I photograph ok," I let out a nervous chuckle.

"Chante, you are beautiful. You are very photogenic. I am going to have you looking like a true boss in these pictures. I cannot wait for you to see these shots at the end. Trust me, you will definitely enjoy them."

"In that case, let's get to work then!"

We all took our places and the shoot began. Nia was a master with a camera. She placed me and gave great instructions on what she was looking for me to do and what she wanted to capture for the magazine photos. I could tell I was a little tense at first because Nia kept telling me to relax my shoulders and 'act natural'. It was hard at first, but once she told me to just act like I was at work on a normal day doing what I loved, it was like second nature. Nia was a great photographer, and she knew how to work a camera. The shoot was very laid back and I was able to just completely be myself in all of the shots. They took pictures of me outside of my office, inside, and a few model-type shots in an area that we had set up.

After the shots were done, Nia let me sit down and look at all of them and pick the ones I would want for the magazine. She even took shots of me during the interview. Having that kind of control really made me feel like I had finally arrived. It lived up to every one of my expectations. Even my headshots were amazing. Nia really did go above and beyond to make these pictures the best they could be.

After my photoshoot was done, I sat down for my interview, which was also as natural as a conversation that I had been having with a friend for years. The shoot and interview took about four hours, but it was well worth the time. I felt like at the end, we got a lot of quality work done. I was very pleased at the end of it and could not wait until it came out so I could read it.

After everyone was wrapping up and going home, I noticed Nia stuck around afterwards.

"Hey Nia, what's up? Something wrong?" I said.

"No, no! I really feel like such a groupie doing this, but I am not sure when I would be able to see you again in this lifetime. I wanted to know if you could sign all of my copies of your books before I left?"

I blushed a little, "Sure! I wouldn't mind at all!" I saw her face light up as she grabbed her books out of her bag; eager for me to sign. With no hesitation, I grabbed my autograph pen out of my desk and began signing each one.

Nia sat in front of me, grinning from ear to ear, "I feel like such a groupie, but I knew that if I was going to be with you all day, why not try and get autographs while I could? I've never had autographed copies of any of the books I have. You're the first author I've got to sign books for me!"

"You are way too kind! I may need to keep you around if you're going to gas me like this!" I said. It had been a long time since I had someone else besides my mother rooting for me. Liyah used to be that person for me, but of course, she's not that person anymore.

"No problem! The way I see it, we as young women and creatives need to continue to keep ourselves uplifted; if nothing more, between each other, because we all know that no one else is doing it," she said.

I proceeded to sign all of her books and took a photo with

her as well. We chatted about our work and personal lives before we decided to eventually call it a day. I told Nia to make sure she sent me a signed copy of that photo so that I could hang it in my office.

"I want to be able to tell people I know and had my first professional magazine shoot by the world-famous Nia Maxwell someday."

"Bet!" she said. "It was truly a pleasure meeting you, Chante. I hope we can meet up again soon. If you ever need some photos done..."

"You will be the first person I call," I said.

Today was a great day; one of the greatest days of my professional career. Without having Liyah and Tara in my corner, I longed for some female companionship. Spending the day shooting with Nia and her team made me feel confident and excited for what was to come of my career, and Nia was a great person to talk to. We exchanged numbers because I knew I could use her for more work in the future and who knows, maybe we could even be friends?

FOUR

I was pretty well-known in the writing industry, especially now that my interview hit all of the coffee shops, bookstores and newsstands. The morning it came out, Nia had texted me a picture of the cover, and the spread that was featured in the magazine. Her caption said, "I think we might be famous now." I smiled instantly. She really knew how to brighten my mood. She came right over to my house with a stack of copies that she wanted me to sign that she was going to hand out to people so they would have an autographed copy of my article. Nia was always about exposure and making connections. That's what I liked most about her; she knew a lot of people and was willing to share her success with others to help them be successful as well. With me still getting on my feet and trying to get my name out in DC as a publishing company, every little bit helps. So along with her professional connections, she was also just a cool chick to be around.

Needless to say, Nia and I became fast friends after we first met. The more we spent time together, the more we realized we had a lot more in common than we imagined. We were able to connect in different ways personally and professionally. She recently reached out to me about a party that she was going to, which was similar to a networking event in downtown DC. She thought it would be a good place for me to go and meet some other writers in the area and link with other black creatives in DC. She was the type of friend that was supportive of your career and did everything she could to help herself and others get ahead and she knew the importance of networking.

It almost felt like Nia and I were cut from the same cloth. Our experiences were almost a bit similar, so we could identify with a lot of the experiences we each went through, and how important it was for us to be successful at the point we were at in our lives. I was one year older than her, but we seemed to have come from similar backgrounds. We were both pretty chill in high school and college; both obviously very creative spirits. She also had a daughter that was about a year and a half younger than Chelsea. Naturally, I didn't let her know everything right at the beginning, but I figured in time, maybe I could let her know all of my deep, dark secrets. I did tell her that I was recently divorced, but luckily, she didn't pry about the details. I'm glad she didn't want to know too much, because I wasn't sure if I was ready to tell. I told her that the situation was still fresh, and I did tell her that his new wife and I were not on good terms. Eventually, I'll explain to her the sordid ordeal that happened between Liyah and I.

Nia let me know about her relationship history, which involved her daughter Mariya's father, Kevin. Nia said that she and Kevin were high school sweethearts, and that they went to different colleges, but stayed connected throughout. She said that she got pregnant right before she graduated grad school, and at first Kevin was happy about it, but as the time was drawing near for Mariya to be born, he became more and more distant. She tried to get him to be excited about it, but she could tell that he was questioning the idea of being a parent. Pretty soon, Mariya was here, and Kevin was nowhere to be found. She said after three months he came back around, claiming he was 'shook about being a father' and that he was ready then. They tried to make a relationship work, but it was forced, and he began to fade in and out again. After that Nia told him to either stay in her life or get out, but he didn't need to play games, especially now that they had a child to think about. He decided to stay out, but he does pay his child support on time, which is more than what she can say for some of her friends' baby's fathers. I could tell Nia was disappointed in Kevin's decision not to be present in Mariya's life, but it was his choice to make, and she vowed to make sure she would provide for her child and make sure she had everything she could ever ask for and more. She never wanted her daughter to feel like she couldn't have, just because she came from a single-parent household. "I watched my mother struggle, and I don't want that for Riya. So I bust my ass for her, ya' know?"

"I feel you, Nia. You do a great job for her. You're a bomb ass mother; don't let anyone take that from you."

When Chelsea returned from Florida, I was able to let her meet Mariya; and just like Nia and I, they clicked instantly. Chelsea was so happy to have a new friend in DC to play with and it made me feel good for her to have a new friend as well. It felt like after so long, things were falling into place for us.

Now that Chelsea was back, we could get back into the full swing of things and get ready for the upcoming school year. It always felt better when she is with me. When she returned, she told me all about the things she and her father did over the summer; how she played with TJ, and how her "auntie Liyah" would act. She was still very unfamiliar to how everything played out, but she tried to roll with the punches the only way a six-year-old knew how. I knew how difficult the transition that Liyah made in her life was, and I felt guilty at times that I couldn't really explain a lot of what happened to her; only because she was not really old enough to understand truly what was going on between her father and I.

One of the things I know Chelsea missed was having someone closed to her age to play with, which is why introducing Chelsea to Mariya was a good idea. As soon as they met, they would've spent every waking moment together if Nia and I let them, and they even had several sleepovers during the weekends. They had a few more to enjoy before school started, so we decided to let them at least enjoy them together.

One Friday afternoon, we were letting Mariya and Chelsea play together; something that had become our new summer routine. Nia and I sat down under a tree and watched our children play on the playground.

"So, what's on the agenda for this weekend?" Nia asked.

"Nothing much really. I have some editing to do, and I have to start packing for this trip to LA next week. My mom is coming up here on Tuesday to keep Chelsea while I am on this trip, then I have a small break but then I will be planning on being gone for a couple weeks while I hit a few more cities on the West Coast. Normally I would let Trey keep her, but I don't want her missing any school."

"Damn girl, the West Coast? That's dope!" Nia said, "Mariya is going to miss Chelsea while you're gone."

"Well, I told my mom about you and Mariya and how she loves hanging out with her. I already told her that if she needed a break to call you to get Chelsea, so she can have a break. But please if you can keep Chelsea, come get her so my mom can have a break from her. She won't admit it, but I know she wears her out sometimes, and she will need a break," I said.

"That's great! I'll make sure to get your mom's number from you. At this point, if we let them go a weekend without playing with each other, they'll hate us forever!" she said. We both laughed.

"So, enough about work, let's talk about that date you went on the other night. What happened with that?" Nia was looking at me with googly eyes. I knew she was going to want to know how that went.

Nia had bugged me about getting on a dating app to try and get out there and finding someone to date; and even though I really wasn't trying to hear that shit, I tried it out anyway. It's been two years since I had been in a relationship, and Trey has clearly moved on and left no room for the thought of him leaving Liyah and coming back to me (not that I had considered that ever happening or anything), so I decided to focus on getting back into the dating world. The way Nia put it, *Chante you at least need somebody to keep you warm at night.* I guess she was right. So far, I've been on four dates and it was the most horrible experience, and I regretted the shit I did to Trey every time I had a bad date.

"Girl, this shit is for the birds! I mean, these guys around here have nothing going for themselves, and they just want to fuck. I am too old for booty calls and to be carrying a man who don't do shit for himself. I don't understand how men became so problematic. The whole idea of dating sucks now," I said, taking a sip of my water.

Nia looked at me and was laughing, "Well, I told you what you were getting into with these guys. There are very few men out here worth taking a good look at these days; hell, it's why I gave up men in the first place. You probably should too."

I looked at Nia and laughed, "I think there is still hope for me, Nia. I'm not going to give up men."

"Shit, your loss."

I remember when Nia first told me she was a lesbian. She was very discreet about it at first, and admitted that she didn't want to tell me. She feared that I would feel some type of way about her, and not want to be friends. She told me that she has actually lost friends because of it, and I thought that was the most insane bullshit I had ever heard. I quickly told her that we were way too old for that type of mentality, and that whatever her preferences were didn't bother me. I told her that I wasn't that type of friend, and anyone who treated her like that didn't deserve to be her friend in the first place.

After that, she became a lot more open with me, knowing that I was comfortable with her lifestyle. She said after breaking up with Kevin, she tried to get out there and date, but was only faced with more heartbreak. She realized the more she was out in the dating world, she found herself being more and more attracted to women. She tried to fight the attraction, but finally, after meeting a woman at a party she couldn't fight the attraction; she just said 'fuck it' and tried dating her. The relationship didn't last long, but she knew from that point forward that she felt more comfortable dating and being with women romantically. Ever since then, that is how she identified, and she hasn't looked back since.

Nia sipped her water and said, "If you say so, sis; but if you ever change your mind, I will take you out for a Saturday night in my neck of the woods," We both laughed.

Later that evening, Chelsea was already fast asleep from the day, and I decided to start packing and preparing for my trip to Los Angeles on Wednesday. I was in my bedroom with my music blasting and dancing in my closet. I was throwing clothes from my closet to my bed; trying to find the perfect pieces to take with me to LA for the events that I had planned as I listened to the music transition from one song to the next. The song changed and *A Couple of Forevers,* by Chrisette Michele began to play through my speakers.

The song made me pause; my mood shifted from joy to sadness. A song that once brought joy to my heart and a smile to my face, now just cuts like a knife. *"Damn,"* I thought. I remember the night I played this song like it was yesterday. I had the song playing on repeat one night when Trey came home from work. I told him that I would feel like this for him for the rest of my life. It was right after we were getting back on the right track and the song fit my emotions for him perfectly, despite all the shit I had done. Now, I know the song means nothing to him, and not much to me either.

I walked over to my phone, opened up Apple Music and deleted the song from my 'Favorites'. I couldn't take it. It was still too emotional to listen to right now; and maybe when I'm ready, I'll add it back to my playlist. I scrolled through my songs and found another song to play, turned it up and tried to shift my mood back to something a little more uplifting while I finished packing. Once I got to a decent stopping point for the night, I put my suitcase in the closet for the night and got ready for bed. I think I had done enough traveling down memory lane for one night. I would finish packing up for my trip tomorrow.

FIVE

A few days later, one of my dreams was coming true. I was finally on the West Coast, promoting my new book release. Being in Los Angeles was a great experience and I had a great turnout. I spent four productive days in Los Angeles, and although there wasn't too much time for play, the work was worth it. The book signing was held at The Last Bookstore in Los Angeles, which has been on my bucket list since I could read. The workshop and reading that we held were filled with positive vibes and great energy. Everyone that works there is very friendly, and the style is just what I look for in a bookstore. I loved interacting with my fans as much as I can and when I do tours or workshops, we are always able to have great discussions around the issues in my books. I even got to do a few previews of some new projects that we had coming up in the upcoming year. Everyone was just as excited as I was to see the new talent I had on board.

The entire day was filled with me signing books, taking pictures, conducting interviews and Q&A sessions about business ventures, entrepreneurship and self-publishing. I was buzzing the entire day. This was where I felt the most alive; when I'm knee-deep into my work. Writing has and always been a passion of mine; and being in the field that I went to college for is no something everyone gets to do every day. I've always been honored to have this privilege.

I couldn't believe how many people had come to the workshop. It always shocked me when I could see a packed house of women of color show up to an event; pen and paper in hand, ready to take notes and learn about my experiences and take any wisdom I had to offer. There were women there of all ages, background and experiences and it felt great to get to speak with everyone.

After the workshop and the question and answer session, many women came up to me thanking me for speaking. I had been able to talk about some of the struggles I had went through (going through my depression and my divorce and how that effected my work ethic), and several women were able to either relate to that or take advice on how to thrive from that.

I began to set up for the book signing after that. I saw the swarm of people line up to get one, two or all three of my books signed at once. There were fans, young and old, and across all demographics that continued to shower me with praise and their own personal testimonials about how my books had impacted their lives in such a positive way. I knew that from all the smiling I had done that day, my face would be sore for a week.

About mid-way through the signing, as I stood up to take a picture with a fan, I just so happened to see a face I haven't seen in years. As I focused my eyes on him, I immediately knew who it was; an old friend from college; Anthony Bishop.

When I saw him, I almost couldn't believe it was actually him. It has been years since I had seen Anthony, and here he was standing right in front of me, waiting on getting a book signed! The last thing I heard about him was that he was married and living in Los Angeles with his wife, from what I gathered the last time I checked out his Facebook page. I never thought of seeing him at a book signing. He never seemed like the type to have his nose buried in a book when we were in college, he was always the first one down to party, though.

There were about four people ahead of him, and as the distance between us began to get shorter and shorter, we made slight eye contact. He shot me a goofy smile and I laughed. As I signed the customers book ahead of him, we were face to face. Once he was next in line, he moved in to smother me in a hug.

"Ms. Chante Thomas. I can't believe I'm seeing you again

after all these years."

"Hey Anthony! I cannot believe it's been so long! How have you been doing?"

"I can't complain. I had heard you were going to be in town doing a book signing and I had to come get my books signed. I've been following you since you first published. You are an amazing writer, girl! Congratulations on all your success!"

"Thank you so much, Anthony. I appreciate you so much for that, really," I said. He flashed me the prettiest smile I've seen in a long time. His teeth were perfect.

Anthony was still as fine as he had always been since college. It had been a long time since we had seen one another, but the years had been very good to him. I could tell he was also admiring me as well.

"Damn girl! You're still looking good after all these years. How do you do it?"

"I try to eat right, and I work out like, every day. But I'm definitely not perfect, so I'm glad someone notices the work I put in! I must say you don't look half bad yourself," I said.

I let my eyes scan him for a quick minute. He was slightly shorter than Trey, and his skin was flawless. He had a clean-shaven bald head and perfectly shaped goatee. He looked like he had just stepped out of the barber chair, and I loved when a man was freshly groomed. The one thing that I could never stop staring at was his eyes. Anthony had deep brown eyes that you could get lost in. They were beautiful. He was also very fit, I could see his muscles popping out of the sleeves of his black V-neck T-shirt. Yea, post grad life had served him well. As I began to get lost in this beauty, I let my eyes wander down to his midsection where I could get a nice print to see if Anthony truly was packing, but he snapped me out of my trance.

"So, are you going to sign my book or are we going to keep holding up the line? I think the ladies behind me are talking about us," He said chuckling.

I immediately got myself together and sat back down. "Oh sure! Sorry," I said awkwardly. *"how awkward can you be, Chante?"* I thought to myself. I could tell it had truly been a long time since I had gotten any, because in five minutes I was already imagining Anthony taking me in the back room of this bookstore and fucking me silly. I couldn't help it though; the man is fine!

As I took his books from him, I began to put my signature in the front cover. I looked up at him smiling, and he was smiling right back at me.

After I signed his book, I handed it back to him and decided that I would make a move. What the hell? What's the worst that could happen, right?

"So, I would regret it forever if I didn't offer to meet up somewhere and catch up. It's been so long and it's nice to see a familiar face on these tours. Are you free later on tonight? Unless there is something or someone that's got you tied up this evening?"

Anthony looked at me and said, "Well, I don't have anyone or anything tying me up tonight, so that sounds great! I would love to catch up! I have got to hear about how everything with my favorite couple has been going."

I felt the hairs stand up on the back of my neck because I hadn't realized that Anthony is going to be in for a treat when he finds out that Trey and I aren't together, *"Well this is going to be interesting,"* I thought. I decided that I wouldn't reveal any of the details until we were more on a one-on-one setting. I also noticed he did mention the word 'tonight'. I'll be sure to pick his brain as well.

"Well, alright! Let's meet back up here around eight. I will let you show me a good time in these LA streets. So, you better impress me, Mr. Bishop," I said chuckling.

"Perfect! I think I have the perfect spot for us to hang out. I think you'll like it."

I exchanged numbers with Anthony just so I can let him know when I got back to the bookstore and he left, and I continued to manage the wave of people who had come to see me and have their books signed.

Once I got done at the book signing, I took a car back to the hotel, and prepared to get ready to go out with Anthony. I decided to call Nia to give her the details. She would be happy to know I found someone to hang out with out here.

I called her on Facetime.

"Hey girl," She said. She was editing on her computer when I called. "Hey, Nia. Do you want me to call you back?"

"Nah. I am just editing a few photos. What's up? How was the book signing? Tell me all about it!"

"It was actually awesome! The crowd was great! There were almost people outside that couldn't get in. I was so overwhelmed with happiness."

"Chante, that is amazing!! I told you that LA was going to show you a lot of love. People love you on the West Coast. They love the arts out there."

"I know; you did say that. You're always right, my Nia. But guess what?"

"What's up?"
"Soooo, I met an old friend while I was at the book signing. I'm actually getting ready to meet him to hang out."

Nia instantly stopped what she was doing and looked at her

phone, "Shut the fuck up! Are you serious?! Girl! What's his name?"

I laughed hysterically. She's crazy, "his name is Anthony Bishop. I went to college with him actually. I haven't seen him in a long time, and he was right there at my book signing today."

"Well, what did he say? How did he look?"

"I mean the conversation was light and quick because we didn't want to hold up the line at the bookstore. And girl, he looked fine as hell. I haven't seen him in a while, but he was looking good enough to eat. I forgot how fine he was."

"Aww shit now, Chante. Go on and get your groove back girl! I love this! Where are y'all going?"

"I'm not sure. He told me he was going to take me somewhere that he thinks I would like out here. I'm going to meet him at the bookstore and then we are going to go from there. I'm excited to see where the night ends up."

"Well girl, have fun, be safe and make sure he wears a condom."

I looked at the phone and rolled my eyes, "girl if you don't shut the hell up," I laughed.

Nia laughed too, "I'm just being honest. You never know what might happen. YOLO girl; do people even still say that?"

"Whatever Nia. I gotta go. How does my outfit look?"

I took my phone and scanned my outfit. I had on a red crop blouse with black pants and sandals. I wanted to be casual, but cute, since I didn't know where we were going. I kept my hair down and framing my face like it was at the book signing. My makeup was subtle with a sultry smoky eye.

"You look perfect! I love it!"

"Great. Alright. Gotta go. I love you; I'll call you later with details."

"Bye girl; love you too," Nia said.

We hung up. I took one more look at myself in the mirror, touched up my lipstick and I was on my way.

A couple of hours later, I was standing outside of the bookstore, waiting for Anthony. I was sitting down on the bench outside of the entrance, slightly fidgeting and tapping my foot nervously. I kept looking at my outfit, wondering if I should've dressed up more for the occasion, *"I hope he doesn't think I look busted."* I thought. Soon, I saw him walking up to me, and I immediately felt like a freshman going out with the finest upperclassman on campus.

"Hey there, miss lady!" he said, with a beaming smile on his face.

"Hey! You ready?"

"Yes. Let's go; I'm starving."

"Me too."

He looked even better than he did in the bookstore. He was wearing a black button up shirt and light jeans. He had on a pair of shades and I could smell his cologne; which was making me weak. He walked with some LA swag and confidence that was so damn sexy.

He looked over to me and asked, "So, are you ready to go? I have a reservation for us at one of the best places to eat in Los Angeles. You'd love it."

"Sure! Let's go!" I said. He reached out for my hand and I placed my hand in his. He pointed and stated that the place he wanted to go was close to the bookstore, so we decided to take a nice stroll since the weather was perfect.

The bistro we went to was the cutest thing! We picked a spot outside on the patio dining area where we could see the sunset. We started out with drinks and appetizers and started to catch up on all the things that have gone on in the years between now and college graduation. Anthony told me how he was in a serious relationship with this girl he met after he graduated; they were even engaged. It turned out she had some issues going on and she was very insecure about herself and their relationship. He said she really never trusted that he was only in love with her.

"I had to let her go. It was very hard for me to do, but I am a better man for it. We even still talk on occasion; I check in on her to make sure she's alright. Even though our relationship did not work, I always wanted to make sure she knew that she had someone who cares about her if she needed, ya know? So, we remain good friends to this day."

"That is very sweet of you, Anthony. You know guys these days will drop you like a bad habit and not even care if you're still making it in life. It's nice to know that you are still there for her," I said.

"So, how have you been, Chante? Aside from being a famous author and all?" Anthony asked me as he sipped his coffee.

I paused for a moment to think about my options here. I could lie to him about everything that went down between Trey and I, or just say we aren't together anymore. I could also put it all on Trey and say he was a lying cheating bastard. *"Well, that will lead to harsh ass karma, Chante,"* I thought. I don't want to wish any negative vibes on Trey because it wasn't his fault. I decided to play coy and offer up as little information as I could. I took a sip of my drink and used my words cautiously.

"Well, work has been far more successful than I ever imagined. I had always dreamed of publishing and writing; and if you want me to be honest, I didn't think it would happen for me. I thought I would have some office job somewhere, regretting my decision to not take the risks and do what I'm passionate about.

But I put in the work, and here I am. It's all still surreal sometimes, but I truly love what I do. I wouldn't say famous just yet, but I'm pretty well-known in some pretty important circles and that is enough for me."

"Oh ok. I like that; a woman who is driven and passionate. How about you and Trey?" he inquired.

I took another sip of my drink, and replied, "Well, we were doing well for the first two or three years of our marriage, but after a while, we began to grow apart. I'm not proud of it, but I wasn't faithful while we were married, and now, we're divorced," I said. *"No need to tell him about the whole obsessive suicide victim, emotionally abusive fling and the best friend getting knocked up by my husband as revenge part,"* I'm sure that's way too much on a first date that I can't even really consider a date yet anyway.

Anthony sat back in his chair and looked at me, "wow! I never would have thought you guys wouldn't have made it. You guys were 'relationship goals', or whatever," he said laughing slightly. "And don't beat yourself up about what has happened between you guys; honestly, shit happens. People do worse things to their spouse every day. You just have to learn from what you have experienced and know how to solve those problems in a positive way the next time."

Hearing those words from Anthony were honestly really refreshing. It felt so good to not be judged by someone for once. Only certain people and family members truly know what happened between us; and I try to keep it under wraps with a lot of others who I know.

"Thanks, Anthony. It has definitely been rough. And co-parenting up and down the East Coast is not really how we thought our lives would be going, but we are making it work and trying to be as civil as possible. It's working, just not the life I had in mind."

"Well, I'm sure you're doing the best you can."

"Anyways, Mr. Bishop; you have learned a lot of things about me today, but I've heard nothing about you and your success. Tell me what you have been up to."

"Well, I've been in advertising and marketing for some time now. My firm is one of the best ones here in the state of California. And living here isn't so bad either; the weather is always nice, and I live very close to the beach. It's definitely grown on me over the last few years."

"Well, I am also very happy and proud of you too," I said. *"Damn. Smart and fine. Who is this unicorn?"* I thought to myself. Anthony was something straight out of a damn fairytale book these days.

"So here we are; two single, successful black millennials doing quite well for ourselves."

I noticed he made sure to emphasize the word single. He smiled at me and we continued to drink our coffee and chat.

"I guess you're right. Very successful, black millennials, huh?"

"You forgot I said single, too," he said with a smirk.

I looked over the rim of my glass, "I heard you loud and clear, Anthony."

As our evening came to a close, Anthony took me back to the bookstore so that I could get my car.

"So, it was really nice catching up with you, Chante. It was definitely good seeing you after all those years," Anthony said as he walked me over to my car.

"It was nice seeing you too, Anthony."

As I grabbed my keys and attempted to open my door, Anthony tapped me on the shoulder, "so, do you mind if I hit you up sometime? You know, just to catch up and keep in touch?"

Without hesitation, I said, "I would like that."

"It would be refreshing to hear from you every now and then."

I smiled at him as I pulled a card out of my bag, "this has my phone number and email on it, so you have an option to choose however you want to contact me."

"Cool. I guess I'll give you one of my cards also, in case you want to make the first move."

He was smooth; I'll give him that. Anthony was always good at flirting. I was just too smitten by Trey to really pay any attention to it. I took his card and said, "I'll take good care of it."

We gave each other a hug; one that lasted just long enough for me to remember it until the next time I heard from him again. He smelled so good I almost didn't want to let go. He had on just the right amount of cologne; not too overpowering to the point where it might kill me. It was just enough to linger and have me thinking about it all night long.

I got in my car and waved good-bye to Anthony. He waved back and then went to his car once he saw I was safely driving away. On the way back to my room, I couldn't stop giggling and smiling. I was texting Nia telling her all the details of what happened. She asked me if he tried to get some and I told her no; "he was a perfect gentleman." This was not what I was used to since I've been on the dating scene. To have a real man take me out, and not expect anything at the end of the night was very hard to come by these days. I'm glad I found it in Anthony. I don't think I've felt butterflies in my stomach after a date in a long time; and I was hoping that even though we were thousands of miles, maybe he could give me a few more reasons to travel back to the West Coast.

SIX

It had been about three days since my trip back from LA, and my mind was still on my date with Anthony. I had a quick pit stop back home before I had to take a few more trips, and everyone kept talking about how great the trip went. I was excited about it as well, but they didn't know about my extracurriculars. Our evening together was great, and we promised to keep in touch with each other, although we were a whole nation away. I was hoping that was a true statement.

I was close to being done with my tour, I had a few events left before I'd finally be home and back to my normal life. I loved what I did, but being at home was probably the one thing I missed the most. I wanted to see Chelsea and get back to being in my element and doing what I really loved the most, which was writing. I had a few ideas I wanted to get started on, and I had already scheduled a meeting with my agent for when I got home, so I was anticipating that more than anything.

I was sitting in my hotel room one night after an event, getting ready to turn in for the night when I noticed an envelope icon waiting for me in the corner of my screen. I initially didn't pay it any mind; it was probably Nia sending me something crazy like she always does, or even something about work that I could deal with in the morning. Then, it hit me, *what if it's Anthony?* I immediately clicked on the envelope to see what it said.

To: Chante Thomas < cThomas@gmail.com >
From: Anthony Bishop < anthonybsmooth@yahoo.com >
Time: 9:30 pm
Subject: Nice to see you

Hey Chante,

I've been debating on when I was going to send this email; and I figured with you being such a busy woman, calling you might not have been the best idea. So here I am, making the first move (lol). I just wanted you to know that I really enjoyed spending that time with you while you were in LA. Kind of felt like old times running into an old friend ☺ . I hope this message finds you in good spirits, and I hope to hear from you soon.

-Ant

When I got finished reading it, I could tell I was blushing a bit. He was right, it brought me back to our college days when we would hang out and laugh all night. The only difference between that lifetime and now, is that Trey is no longer in the picture. I decided to sit down and send him an email back before I got into my writing.

To: Anthony Bishop < anthonybsmooth@yahoo.com >
From: Chante Thomas < cThomas@gmail.com >
Time: 11:00 pm
Subject: RE: Nice to see you

Hey Anthony!

I was playing a little hard to get and making you sweat, but I hope I didn't scare you away ;). I also had a great time and it felt so good catching up with you! Hopefully, if you're ever in the DC area we can meet up again and catch up some more!

-CT

P.S – Sorry I am getting back to you so late, I had a long day today, but the tour is almost over.

"I hope I don't sound too corny", I thought to myself. I haven't flirted with a man in years. After Channing, I hadn't even looked in the direction of a man in a while. I had started to casually date, but I realized that conversation and flirting were a lost art. After that I decided to just stay single and preserve what I had left of my tolerance for men. Seeing Anthony's fine ass made me remember what it was like to actually like a guy.

To: Chante Thomas < cThomas@gmail.com >
From: Anthony Bishop < anthonybsmooth@yahoo.com >
Time: 11:30 pm
Subject: Re: Nice to see you

Lol, I didn't realize you would be up at this hour! I was hoping you wouldn't see my corny email until in the morning (haha). Since you brought it up though, I have been thinking about visiting the DMV. I have always wanted to travel back to the East coast, but never really had a reason to go further than the Midwest. I guess now, I can say I have a pretty good reason ;). Let me check out some dates on my end and I can plan to come see you again, if that's not too forward; because I would love to see you again very soon.

-Ant

P.S. – and you're fine. I know that is your passion, as long as you didn't forget about me ;).

I was sitting in my bed giggling at my Mac like a little schoolgirl. Part of me couldn't believe that he was this sweet; and then he sounded too good to be true.

"Well, the ball is in my court now. I need to make a decision as to whether he is going to come see me or if I'm going to blow him off," I thought. He seems like he is willing to get to know me and I would definitely love to get to know more of him.

To: Anthony Bishop < anthonybsmooth@yahoo.com >
From: Chante Thomas < cThomas@gmail.com >
Time: 12:05 am
Subject: RE: Nice to see you

Well, I don't think that would be a bad idea at all. It is not forward of you to ask, and it also gives me a good reason to come see the beautiful city of LA again. Let's check our calendars and throw out some dates and see what sticks, ok? 😊

-CT

"There, it's done," I thought. I figure if I ever want to get out of the shallow end, I need to show a bit of assertiveness. He told me that he would check his calendar and send me a few options.

"We'll see."

Three long days later, I was finally home. Anthony and I had moved from emails to text messages through the latter part of my trip and my traveling. It was nice to come off of a long flight, turn on my phone and see a message from him. I forgot how fun flirting could actually be! When I got home, my mother was there with Chelsea, and Nia was there too with Mariya. Chelsea ran up to me and squeezed me so tightly I thought she was going to suffocate me. I didn't realize how much she missed me, and I missed her just as much; if not more. My mom let me get settled, and decided she was going to cook dinner. While my mother cooked, I told Nia about my long night of emailing with Anthony. She tried to clown me at first, because we chose to email each other out of all things.

"Seriously? Emailing? Who emails anymore, Chante?" she said laughing in between her sentences.

"We do, Nia! Shit, I'm not even the one who sent the first one; he did. I think he did it because he wasn't expecting me to see it until the next day. If I would have gotten a text from him, I would have seen it immediately. Either way, I thought it was cute. Plus, it was a lot easier because I wasn't even paying attention to my phone all day and when I got to my hotel, I started to do some writing on a project, so it was easier that way," I said throwing my pillow at her.

"So, is he really going to come visit?" she asked.

"He said he would. We're supposed to be looking at different dates to see what matches up with our schedules. He seems serious about it because when I came off the plane, I had a text message with like three or four different weekend options on it. I think he really wants to come out here."

"Oh, so he can text," Nia said sarcastically. She stuck her tongue out at me and I rolled my eyes as I sipped my water.

"Bitch, don't hate."

The next morning, Anthony and I confirmed that he would come see me about three weeks from now. Once I confirmed it, I felt a slight feeling of apprehension. I didn't want Anthony to be just another handsome face, but I took a chance. Something about him felt different. No sooner than I confirmed, Anthony said that he would purchase a ticket and send me the confirmation. So, I had three weeks to get myself prepared for my second date with him. Each time I felt like I was going back to square one, but something about Anthony felt so different, so I hoped for the best.

Later that day after lunch, I was online shopping for a couple of new outfits to choose from for my date when I probably should have been working. I didn't know exactly what look I wanted to go with, so I decided on several different options and continued to pile things into my cart to purchase. My assistant came into my doorway, and I was so into what I was doing I didn't hear her call my name the first time.

"Ms. Thomas?"

I snapped out of my trance, "oh, yes? Sorry. I didn't even realize you were there."

"It's ok," she said with a nervous-like chuckle, "I wanted to get your final edits on the agenda for the conference call we are having about the winter writer's retreat workshop so I can prepare them. Should I come back later or..."

"Oh shit, Stacy. I forgot all about those edits. When is this call again? I don't know why I put so much on myself sometimes."

"It's on Thursday. And come on Ms. Thomas; if you want to be the next Toni Morrison or Terri McMillan, you have to do these kinds of things."

I looked up at my portrait and quote of the great Ms. Morrison and sighed, *"A legend's work is never done."*

"Stacy, give me an hour and I'll have it ready for you."

Looks like my date planning would have to wait at least an hour so I can get some real work done right now.

SEVEN

"Ok, you got this. It's just a date. No need to be so nervous."

The day had finally come. I was going on my first date with Anthony since I had seen him in LA.

This is what I continued to remind myself as I let my GPS lead me to my destination to meet Anthony. You would think I was 16 and this was the first date I had ever been on, but I was just that nervous.

He told me to meet him at a specific location, and then he would take me to dinner. "I want to surprise you," he said; so I obliged, as much as I don't truly care for surprises. He was lucky I trusted him at this point, because if he was anyone else, I would've thought he was crazy as hell and wouldn't have went. I figured he was trying to impress me, so I gave him the chance to see what he could really do.

The last three weeks had the anticipation mounting day by day. Anthony refused to tell me any part of what he had planned for our date. I had known that he flew in, but wouldn't stay at my place, out of respect for Chelsea being there. Even though I offered to let her stay with Nia, he declined. "I don't want to have the first trip I take down here to be laid up in your house. I'm going to respect you, so I am going to stay at a hotel."

He told me that he had a very specific evening planned and had to make some big choices because he didn't get to have as much time as he planned to come, so he wanted to make the most of it. I was perfectly content with sending naughty emails via cyberspace with him and letting it be just that, but the more I talked to Anthony, the more I began to like him on a deeper level. He was really being a gentleman about this. Could it be that I was actually being courted like a real woman should?

I felt like everything was moving at lightning speed, and I couldn't decide if I liked it or not. The more I wanted to pull away from this, because I didn't think I was ready to date, Nia convinced me to give him a try and see how things go. My worst-case scenario would be that our LA date was a fluke, we would have a bad date, I would put him on the "never in a million years" list with the other guys I've tried to date, and go on about my lonely business.

I was buzzing and my mind was racing the entire time on the drive over. Anthony didn't tell me the actual restaurant we were going to; he only sent me directions. I had never heard of this address, but it wasn't too far from my place.

I turned my music up and continued to get myself amped up for this date. I was so nervous, because I had been out of this game for some years now. Date nights with your husband and date nights with a potential boo are totally different these days.

I pulled up to the spot that my GPS took me to, which was surprisingly accurate. It was right in front of a grocery store. I immediately wondered what was going on, *"I know he isn't taking me on a date to a damn grocery store,"* I thought. After a few moments of frustration and gathering my thoughts to send Anthony a message on how I planned on cancelling, I saw him emerge from the black vehicle sitting a few spaces in front of me. I couldn't believe he had gotten a driver for us for the evening. *"Nice move..."* I thought to myself smiling.

As he walked over to me, I only had one thing to say; *"Damn!"* He was wearing a light blue button up shirt with dark slacks. He was clean shaven, and I could see his pearly white teeth from the car. I took off my seatbelt and got out of my car to greet him. Once I got out, I took a quick minute to smooth out my form-fitting red skirt. I paired that with a navy sleeveless crop top that hit right above my skirt, so that it only showed a small portion of my midsection. I had on my favorite red heels, which were also the most comfortable. Once I gave myself a once-over, I looked up and we made eye contact. He admired my curves while complimenting my outfit.

"I hope I'm not too overdressed for wherever we are going," I said.

"You look perfect," he said. His gaze up and down my frame told me all I needed to know; the outfit was approved.

"So, where are we headed?" I asked in an attempt for him to reveal the location.

"Stop it. I know what you're doing. You'll see when we get there. The only person who knows where we are going aside from me is our driver."

He extended his arm to me so that we could get in his car and head to our destination for the evening.

When we pulled up to the restaurant, I was very impressed. It was a very quiet and quaint place, which means he was listening when I told him I didn't like big fancy restaurants. As we approached, I asked him "How did you find this?"

"Well, I did a little research on the area. I felt like this place would be something you like, so I decided to make us a reservation. They have private dining rooms, so I got us one so that we won't be distracted. It'll just be you and I."

"Wow. All this for me?" I couldn't believe he went through all the trouble of reserving a private dinner room for us. He was aiming to please.

"Yes, and I feel like I wish I could do more, but since we only have tonight while I'm in town, I'm hoping to make a good impression on you," he said with a smile.

We both got out of the car, and Anthony allowed the gentleman to valet his car. When we walked in, I could immediately smell the aroma of Italian food. *"He's definitely been listening to me,"* I thought. I had mentioned in passing conversation that I loved Italian food, and he must have remembered!

Anthony grabbed my hand and escorted me to the area where we will be eating.

"I wanted to make sure you remembered your first date with me, so I had them add some things," he said. Our table was lit by candle, with a large bouquet of roses waiting for me and an invitation to hand pick my choice of wine for the evening. He really outdid himself; and I was impressed.

"Thank you, Anthony. This is so beautiful! I can't believe you went through all this trouble."

"It's like I said; I wanted to make sure I was making a lasting impression. I am pulling out my best moves here, so in case we never work, you can say that I gave you one of the best dates you've been on," he said chuckling.

I smiled at him, as the waiter proceeded to escort me to their wine room, so that I could pick my wine for the evening. I returned to the table and sat down with Anthony. The waiter was behind me with a chilled bottle of white wine.

I couldn't have envisioned a better evening. Anthony was so attentive to me and he knew how to keep a conversation going. We learned so much more about one another, and the food was amazing. Anthony was so easy to talk to and the night was going so well, I didn't realize time was flying by. Before we realized it, we had spent hours in the restaurant. As we were walking out of the restaurant, Anthony made his move.

"So, would you like me to take you straight home? I promise, no funny business; but you've been drinking, and I'd rather have the driver drop you off at home," he said. I couldn't deny that I was definitely buzzed on my way out of the restaurant, but I had to keep my cool because I had made a promise to myself that I wouldn't have sex with him for at least another month.

Anthony could sense my hesitation, as he grabbed my hand and turned me towards him, "look Chante, I know what you may be thinking, and you might think that I am trying to get some tonight. Well, I'm not. As much as I wouldn't mind spending some extra time with you, I really just want to make sure you get home. I will take you to your door, go back to get your car, bring it back and then I will go to my hotel. If I do anything outside of that, then you can never talk to me again," He said with a begging smile.

As much as I hesitated, I decided that if he was willing to go to such lengths, then he must be telling me the truth. I looked into his eyes and said, "Ok." After that, I was ready for whatever.

When we arrived at my apartment, he walked me up to the door. We stood facing each other, just like an awkward first date would end. We both knew what we wanted, but we were too afraid to make the first move. I eventually began the conversation.

"Well, this sounds really cliché, but I really did have an amazing time with you tonight, Anthony. Thank you so much for a wonderful date. It truly was one of the best I've been on in a long time; since Trey actually," I admitted. I couldn't deny the effort that he put into making this date work for us.

"Thank you, Chante. I had an amazing time as well, and I'm glad you enjoyed yourself. I hope this shows you that I am committed to treating you to the finer things, and I hope this gets me another opportunity to take you out."

"You are doing a pretty good job selling yourself, Anthony," I said smiling. "So, we'll see what the future holds."

"I can assure you, it's pretty good," Anthony said.

I looked at him, and suddenly something came over me. I didn't know what I was doing, but suddenly I was asking Anthony to come inside for another drink. *"What the hell?"* I thought. We're both adults and we both know what this is.

"I would love to, Chante, but you know I have the driver tonight; but, if you want me to come up, I can possibly have him head out, and find arrangements to get you to your car and back to my hotel in the morning?" Anthony said. I could tell he was trying to "respect" my wishes of not having him at my home on the first date. My sober mind probably would have told him to go ahead and go, but "tipsy Chante" needed a little more of his company. I wanted to say no, but something inside me didn't want the night to end. Even if we didn't have sex, I was so intrigued by him that I didn't want to stop talking to him.

"I want you to know I'm not doing this to have sex, but I don't want our night to end," I admitted.

"I guess that makes two of us."

After staring in each other's eyes for what felt like an eternity, I could feel our bodies gravitating towards one another. Before I knew it, our lips met one another for the first time.

The kiss was short and sweet, but it was powerful, and damn near knocked me off my feet.

We both pulled away and smiled. I took Anthony's hand and led him through my door to my home, and I allowed the night to take us wherever it was meant to go.

The next morning, I shot up from underneath my comforter. I could immediately feel the headache, courtesy of last night's festivities and realized that whatever went down last night involved too much alcohol.

I immediately looked over to the side of my bed, assuming

Anthony would have been there, but he wasn't. I looked around my room and saw my clothes laid on the edge of my bed. I decided to stretch and try to gather myself enough to make it out of my bed and assess the situation. I knew I could be relieved of one thing; I didn't have sex last night. I climbed out of bed and went into my living room. There was an empty bottle of wine on my coffee table with two glasses, one with a small amount of wine left in it. I looked on my couch and saw Anthony sleeping there. He was still fully clothed and had taken advantage of the blanket I had laying over the couch. He looked so peaceful. I stared at him for a moment, thinking to myself, *"I can't believe he stayed the night, and didn't have sex with me. Hell, I don't even remember him attempting it!"*

I immediately felt guilty automatically assuming that Anthony was all about just getting into my panties and heading back to LA, just to ghost me after all this. I guess he is a little different than other guys. I still had my thoughts, but at least for tonight, I could give him the benefit of the doubt. He was a good guy after all.

I began to gather up the glasses and wine bottle from the table, as I heard him stir in his sleep. I tried to be quiet, so I wouldn't wake him, but I could see him slowly starting to wake.

"Good morning party animal," he said.

"Good morning," I said bashfully, "I see you stayed the night, against my wishes I might add," I said giving him a playful side eye.

He began to sit up on my couch and explain himself, "I know you didn't want me to stay, and I honestly didn't intend to, but I fell asleep and woke up, and you were passed out on the chair. I decided to get you up and put you in your bed, and before I knew it, I was passed back out on your couch. It's pretty comfortable," He said laughing.

I laughed with him briefly, placed my wine glasses in the

kitchen, then went back and sat next to him on the couch.

"I really enjoyed our time last night, Anthony. I'm glad we had time to finish our evening," I said. I really meant it, too, at least of what I remembered of it. I feel like things got a little fuzzy after I popped the cork on that bottle of wine.

At first, I was hesitant about letting him up to my apartment, but after the endless hours of talking and laughing with him, I'm glad I gave him a chance. The best part was that he didn't even try to have sex with me; which I figured was always on every man's mind when they wanted to come up to a lady's apartment. That is at least what I have experienced on my dating adventure in DC so far, and it was far from attractive to me.

"Well, I enjoyed myself as well, Chante. I hope that I made a good first impression on you, and that we get to have more dates like this," he said. I smiled at him and gave him a small kiss on the cheek.

"Here's hoping."

Anthony gathered his wallet and keys and I proceeded to walk him out to his Uber. He had to get back to his hotel and prepare to get on a flight back to LA, where we would continue this long distance...whatever this was. I wasn't sure whether we were officially dating or not, but I do know that I enjoy everything about this man, and I don't plan on entertaining anyone other than him.

As I stood next to the car with him, I said, "I guess I have to say good-bye for now, huh?"

"For now; but don't worry, I will be back sooner than you think."

"I look forward to it."

I leaned in to give him a hug, and he kissed me on the lips long and slow. I wanted to melt into him, but I managed to maintain my balance.

As our kiss ended, he looked at me and said, "I don't know what you're doing to me, Chante Thomas, but I think I like it."

I gave him a seductive smile and gave him another peck on the lips, "you are going to be late for your flight. I'll talk to you soon, Anthony."

He got in the car and drove off, as I waved good-bye. I was floating on a cloud so high; I feel like I practically flew back to my apartment. When I got inside, I sat down on my couch and immediately called Nia to give her all the details. She answered on the second ring.

"Bitch, you fucked him on the first date, didn't you?!" she said. I knew it would probably be one of the first things she asked me.

"Hey Nia, how are you doing?" I said. "And no! What would make you ask me that?"

"Because you would have called me last night so we could talk about the date, but instead you are calling me in the morning, which means you were too busy on your back to call me last night!" she said laughing hysterically.

"Anyway, I did not have sex with Anthony last night. We were so drunk and tired, we both passed out and didn't wake up until this morning; but trust, if I was in a different state of mind, he would've gotten a piece of this last night!"

"Damn, for real?! That's crazy. You know men are always down for some ass to seal the deal on a good date. Not saying you're a random piece of ass, but you know what I mean," She said.

I laughed, "yes, I know what you mean. But surprisingly, it wasn't like that at all. We had a great night; but clearly drank too much, because before I knew it I was on my ass off this alcohol. Overall, he was the perfect gentleman though. It actually makes me like him more that he didn't try anything while I was that drunk."

"That's true. I can tell he knows how to treat women, and he's not a foul ass dog either; so, he's good with me for now."

"Thanks. I live for your approval" I said laughing to myself. "When do you want me to come pick up Chelsea?"

"Whenever you climb out of that euphoria you're in right now, but let's meet up for lunch and then Chelsea can just go home with you after."

"That's fine with me girl. I need you to take me to get my car first." she agreed.

"I'll see you around lunch time," I said and hung up the phone.

I laid back on my bed, and just looked up at the ceiling. Nia was right, I was in great date heaven right now. I was on a high that no one could shake. I felt my phone buzz on the edge of my bed, and I picked it up. It was a text from Anthony.

"Made it with minutes to spare. I guess kissing you really did almost make me late. Wouldn't have minded staying, though."

I smiled and text back, *"now that would have taken me over the moon. But we will see each other again soon, love."*

"Can't wait, baby. I'll call you when I land."

I couldn't help but giggle like a little schoolgirl with a crush. I hadn't felt these types of feelings since I first started dating Trey. It felt good to be wanted again. I was glad our first date went perfectly, because I don't think I want to toss Anthony in the "never in a million years" category at all.

EIGHT

It had been a couple weeks since our first in-person date, and it seems that's all it took to solidify a place in each other's lives. Things between Anthony and I continued to move slow and steady at first, but as we began to get to know each other more and more; the more comfortable I felt taking our relationship to the next level, and it felt really good. Most of our relationship was based via emails, texts, phone calls and a ton of FaceTime; but we made a promise that since we knew this was something we wanted to take seriously, we would invest in seeing each other at least once a month. I knew that my frequent flyer miles were going to rack up at this point.

I had to admit, as nervous as I was about it, I was pretty smitten by him. It felt good to be wanted and pursued after so long of not really having anyone pique my interest seriously and with dealing with all the drama with Trey and Liyah. The more I began to focus my attention on what Anthony and I were trying to build in a serious relationship, the less and less I became concerned with Trey and Liyah.

One day, I was out with Nia, and she wanted to know all about how things were going with Anthony and me. I hadn't seen her in about a month; due to her being out of town for a big photography gig she landed in New York, so I decided to fill her in on everything that has been going on lately.

I was sitting at the table at our favorite brunch spot when she snuck up behind me and surprised me.

"Hey sis! Miss me?" she said.

"Hey Nia! Hell yea I missed you, girl. We have too much to

catch up on! How was New York?"

"It was awesome! The shoot went great and I got some great work done. Even had a couple opportunities to enjoy myself also," Nia said with a slick smirk on her face. I knew exactly what that meant.

"Oh lord! Whose son or daughter did you end up getting with?" I said.

"Girl just one of the stylists I met at the shoot. She is probably only going to be just a lil' fling, which is fine with me. She lives in New York and I'm not down with no long-distance love. I'll keep in touch, but nothing too serious. I'm not you."

Nia sat down and laughed at her own joke. I joined her in laughter, "trust me Nia, I was never this person at first, but Anthony has me doing and feeling things I never have before. I didn't think we would even last past our meeting in LA, but here we are.

The waitress came by our table and asked for our order. We both ordered our food and drinks. After the waitress left with our orders, we proceeded to get into the girl talk.

"So, get to it Chante. What's been going on? How many times have you and Anthony got freaky on FaceTime? When's the wedding? I need details, bitch!

"Whoa, whoa, whoa! Who said anything about weddings? We just decided we were going to be exclusive. I talk to him all the time and I can't get him off my mind at work. We have already started planning for the next time we get together."

"Wow! I hope y'all hurry up and get down to business, because that's how you really know if you're in love or not! Plus, you need to finally get some regular sex in your life, girl. You get a little grumpy when you haven't had a healthy orgasm," Nia said laughing as she took a sip of her margarita.

I threw her the finger and laughed, "kiss my ass, Nia! I'm not even going to get into this with you. But you're right. I do need to release some stress and tension. The last time Anthony was here, I was ready to go there; but he treated me with so much respect, I couldn't even spoil the moment with being some kind of ho."

"I hear that. Well, I'm so happy for you, Chante. I'm so happy for you! You deserve it! So, when's the next time he is going to see you?"

"Since he came down to me, I will have to go to him next time. So, I guess I'll be taking a trip to LA sometime next month." I said. Thinking about it made me a little nervous. I didn't know what our second time seeing each other would be like, but I was beyond ready to see him; in more ways than one.

"Well, let's toast to a successful trip, and lots of fuckin' on the side!" Nia said as she raised her glass.

I took my glass and we engaged in a toast.

Later that night when Chelsea went to sleep, I called Anthony. It had become out nightly routine.

"Well, hello beautiful," He said. His voice was a little raspy, like he had just woken up.

"Hey babe! Were you asleep?"

"Nah, I was just chillin'. I've been waiting on your phone call actually."

"Oh ok. How was your day?"

"It was ok. Nothing special, but with the sound of your voice, my night is looking better." Even through the phone he knows just what to say,

"You really have to stop being like this. You're flattering

me too much."

"It's never enough for you, baby. How was your day?"

I plopped down on the couch got comfortable. I picked up the remote and started scrolling through certain TV shows. I was dressed in my favorite sweats and hoodie, my traditional 'lazy weekend' attire.

"So far, my day was pretty good. I met up with Nia today, she's finally back from her gig in New York."

"Oh, ok. That's what's up. How is she doing?"

"She's good. She had a little too much fun in New York, but I don't blame her," I said chuckling to myself.

"So, speaking of trips, should we start planning for your trip to my side of town? I've been thinking about it lately."

I took a pause and sipped my wine, "I guess we can start tonight. I would be lying if I said I wasn't thinking about seeing you either."

"Well, what are you doing about three weeks from now?" he said. I guess he had already had a date and time in mind.

"Hold on a minute," I pulled my phone down and looked at my calendar. I had a mandatory meeting coming up to discuss some contracts with some new authors, but it didn't conflict with the weekend he was referring to.

"Looks like I'm going to be seeing my boyfriend that weekend," I said smiling.

"Good, because I already booked your flight and I'm emailing you the booking info now." Anthony said. I couldn't believe how forward this man was, but the 'take charge' mentality definitely turned me on.

"Ok then. I guess I'll be seeing you in a few weeks then.

Hopefully, I'll be able to manage just seeing you over the phone until then. Usually I get pretty amped up when I have a special occasion coming up."

"Oh, so now I've been promoted to being considered a special occasion?"

"Absolutely. One of the top priority occasions at that,"

Anthony and I talked on the phone for about another hour. We watched some TV together, making comments and gossiping about the scenes over the commercial breaks. Before I knew it, it was past midnight, and we were falling asleep on the phone. I finally called it a night and went to sleep. While I lay in bed, my excitement and the anticipation of being with Antony in person again kept me awake. I rolled over and shot Nia a text really quickly while the thought was on my mind.

"I'm going to see Anthony in three weeks. Shopping spree?"

I figured this time around, I would make Anthony do a double take, so I wanted to get a few new things, and possibly take a trip to the lingerie store just to seal the deal. Right before I closed my eyes, I heard a *ping* on my phone. I looked over to see what Nia had text me:

"Hell yea! Let's go this week. I'm free on Thursday."

"She never turns down a shopping trip," I thought to myself. I laughed and placed my phone back on the charger, rolled over and fell into Dreamland.

Later that week, while Mariya and Chelsea were at school, I took a half day from work, to begin finding my special wardrobe for my visit with Anthony. I brought Nia along for the ride. I had already notified my office that I would be remote for about four days, two of those days being off limits to work activity. Anthony specifically requested that, so it had me curious as to what he had up his sleeve. Between our FaceTime chatting and text messages, I could tell that absence was making his heart grow fonder and fonder for me. Some of the things he was telling me I needed to hide in a secret folder in my phone for another time.

We went to a boutique Nia shops at frequently and began picking out all sorts of different outfits for my trip. I thought Nia was having more fun than I was with this process. She was picking up all these scandalous outfits that I would never even think of wearing on any other occasion, but she kept insisting.

"Look, I'm trying to get you all the dick you could possibly stand on this trip; and in an outfit like this, Anthony won't know how to keep his hands off you!" she said as she showed me a very low cut and revealing dress.

I had to admit, the dress was fly. I figured with the right shoes I could pull it off on one of our date nights as a surprise. I rolled my eyes and stuck my arm out so she could drape it over, "fine, Nia. I'll try it on. I hope I even look right in a dress like this. It might not even look right on me!"

"Trust me, it will look fine," she said, "now go! And come out when you're done!".

We spent about another two hours trying on clothes and looking at different things until I found some cute outfits I would take with me on my trip to LA. I felt pretty good about my choices, and I kept teasing Anthony between text messages about my choices.

"You're going to be so happy to see everything I picked out," I text him.

"If you're not gonna send pics, don't tease me, boo :'(" he sent back. I wanted to show him really bad, but I decided against it. I figured he needed to be surprised; and surprised he shall be. I couldn't believe the butterflies I was getting about seeing him, but soon we would be spending 4 long days together, and I could not wait.

The next couple of days was filled with what Nia called "the pregame". This meant a full pampering session: manicure, pedicure, eyebrows, hair done, lingerie shopping; and last, but not least, I got a bikini wax. This was something that Nia suggested I do, which was something I had only done once before for Trey; and it hurt like hell.

"Chante! There is no way you can go all the way to the West Coast looking all rough down there. You have to get a wax. Trust me, Anthony will love it!" Nia was doing everything she could to boost me up about this bikini wax, but truth be told, I wasn't feeling it. I was feeling good enough about my mani/pedi I had scheduled the day before my flight. There was nothing more refreshing than me leaving the nail salon with a fresh pedicure and the hair salon with my edges laid; but she insisted, so I figured what the hell? I did it once for Trey, I might as well try it once for Anthony.

Nia booked me an appointment with the spa that does her wax all the time, and she swears by them. I decided that I had time for one more appointment on the day before my flight, so along with getting my mani/pedi and my hair done, I would get the hair-down-there removed too!

"Anthony better enjoy every bit of this," I thought to myself.

The night before my flight, I had packed everything and had my bags by the door. I laid in my bed looking at the ceiling, and very nervous about the trip ahead. This would be the second time Anthony and I had some physical time together, outside of all of our screen time. I was thinking of everything possible that could happen during my trip, all of which hopefully will put Anthony and I in a better position in our relationship; bringing us closer and closer together.

I reached over to my nightstand, took my phone off the charger and opened my messages.

"I'm nervous. What should I expect from this trip?"

I waited a few minutes, until I felt a vibrate from my phone.

"A lot of quality time, and a lot of fun in my town. Why are you trying to get me to reveal my secret plans for you?"

"Because I want to know."

"Well, you can't. What you can know is I will be standing at your gate tomorrow, with a beaming smile because I get to see my queen after two long months. That's all you get so far until tomorrow. Get some rest, baby."

I smiled and put my phone down, *"he's so damn cryptic"* I thought. I left well enough alone for the time being and put my phone back on the charger. He was right, I needed to get some rest because I had to be at the airport hella early.

NINE

As I took my headphones off and watched the plane start to descend into the LAX airport. My heart began to race a little bit. It was like meeting someone for the very first time again. I was a ball of emotions; feeling excited and nervous at the same time. I felt like I didn't know what to expect, even though I knew exactly what I was getting into. I had been around Anthony at least three different times at this point, and I knew what type of guy he was thus far, so there was little to be worried about. I'm hoping the same guy I've been falling for is the same guy who picks me up at the airport today. I've known a lot of things to change once you've spent more time with someone face to face.

No sooner than we were able to turn our phones off airplane mode, I got a message from Anthony telling me he was waiting for me at my gate. I sent him a text telling him we just landed and that I should be with him shortly. They began to allow us to start getting off the plane, so I started to gather my things and head off the plane.

"Well girl, we're here now. No turning back. Let's see what LA and Anthony has to offer you."

I walked off the plane, dressed down in my white T-shirt, skinny ripped jeans, Jordan's and hair pulled back into a neat ponytail. I looked around for a few seconds, and then I saw him. Anthony was standing there looking out the window waiting on me. I smiled and started walking closer and closer to him. He turned and we made eye contact. He looked at me and his smile brightened the entire airport.

"Well, hello gorgeous. Welcome to Los Angeles."

He opened his arms and I fell right into his chest. It felt good to feel him again; to smell his scent again. I was officially in paradise and ready to enjoy a much-needed vacation.

"Hey baby! How are you?"

"I'm great now that you're finally here."

He reached over and wasted no time putting his tongue right into my mouth. The passion behind his kiss was telling of how much he missed me. Absence truly makes the heart grow fonder. He kissed me for what felt like minutes, but I didn't want him to stop. I wanted to do him right in the middle of the airport, but we were in public.

"I've been waiting for this day for a long time, Chante." Anthony said as he finally let me up for air.

"Oh really?"

"Yes."

"Well, I'm glad I was finally able to come see you, babe."

"Definitely. I am going to be the best tour guide/boyfriend you've ever had. By the time your trip is up, you may want to move to the West Coast."

"You're that convincing huh?"

"I am going to do my best to be."

The first stop Anthony and I made was to his place to put some of my things down and freshen up for an early dinner. He lived about 15 minutes from the airport, so it wasn't a long ride at all. The entire time, he held my hand gently. We were so happy to be next to each other we couldn't stop touching. I didn't mind though. I had been in airports and on flights all day and all I wanted to do was eat and spend some quiet time with him.

While we were driving, I couldn't help but feel butterflies

in my stomach. There was something about going to Anthony's home that made me particularly nervous, and I didn't know why. I attributed the feeling to good nerves. The kind you get when you start a new journey and things feel perfect; almost too perfect. I think I was putting a lot on the need for everything to be perfect; just as perfect as it felt in my mind. I tried to shake the feeling and just enjoy the moment that we intended on sharing with each other this weekend.

Anthony noticed the worry in my face and asked me what was wrong.

"Oh nothing baby, I was just enjoying the little bit of sight-seeing we're doing on the road."

"Oh ok; well, I arranged for us to have dinner at my favorite restaurant tonight, so I'm just patiently waiting for that. "

Anthony looked over at me and said, "If we're being honest, I'm a little nervous, and I hope I impress you this weekend! I have a few things for us to do and I hope you're ready."

"I'm definitely ready to see what you have up your sleeve Mr. Bishop," I smiled and continued to look out the window.

When we got to his place, it was completely perfect; almost too perfect, like he had cleaned up right before I got there.

"You're place looks amazing! I really can't believe a man lives here because it's so clean; no offense."

"Oh no offense taken; I know how some brothers are. I have always been pretty organized guy. I can't stand a cluttered space."

Anthony grabbed my bags to take them to his bedroom, "Go ahead and make yourself at home while I put these bags in my room. Do whatever you need to in order to be comfortable."

As he went to his room, I took off my shoes, placed them by the door, and took a seat on his couch. I looked around at his living room, which was very modern. He was a great decorator. He had a deep navy couch and loveseat set, with a glass coffee table in between them. On his table, I saw a Men's Health magazine, and one of my books sitting there. I wondered if he had placed that there purposely, to impress me. When he emerged from his bedroom, he saw me looking at my book.

"So far, it's awesome. I can't put it down. I mean, I'll be taking a break this weekend, because I have the pleasure of having the author in my home; however, once you're gone, I'm diving back into it."

"Really? You like it?"

"Hell yea! It's a page-turner, Chante. You did your thing on that. I can't wait to start the other two."

He turned my head towards him and gave me a long, passionate kiss.

"I'm so happy you're here."

"Well, you did kind of make these plans for me, so how could I turn it down?" I laughed.

"I know. I know it was a bit forward, but I just had to take the chance. I wanted to be a little spontaneous, but also surprise you with not having to pay to come."

He was so generous, and I could see the sincerity in his face, "Anthony, honestly I loved it. I like when a man can go after what he wants and not wait for me to make decisions. You wanted something, and you made the arrangements for me to be here with you, and that was sweet of you."

"I aim to please, baby. Now, let's get ready, we only have about two hours before dinner, and I want to make sure you have enough time to do whatever it is women do to get ready for dates,"

Anthony said.

"Oh shut up, Anthony," I laughed.

He continued to laugh as he entered his bedroom and prepared to shower. "If you want to go ahead and jump in, I have another bathroom across from the second bedroom, babe."

"That's great. Thanks." I gathered my makeup bag and went into the second bathroom.

I turned on my iTunes playlist and got into the mood by dancing and bouncing around the bathroom as I hopped in the shower. When I got out of the shower, I moisturized with my favorite body oil. I sat on the edge of the bathtub, moisturizing my body. The body oil I chose had hints of patchouli oil and citrus. It was my favorite combination. It had been a long time since I was able to get primped and prepped to go out with someone that was actually *worth* going out with, so I pulled out the extra good stuff.

I walked in Anthony's bedroom to get my garment bag. As I looked over into his bathroom, I stole a peek at him in his bathroom, as he was grooming his beard. I let my eyes roam from the top of his head, all the way down his chest. He was damp, so there were small droplets of water still dripping down his chest and stomach. I tried hard to control the fire brewing between my thighs, *"Jesus, this man is fine as hell,"* I thought.

Anthony caught me staring and flashed me a wink and a smile. I smiled back and grabbed my clothes and went to the other room.

"I don't get to see what you're wearing?" He yelled from the bathroom.

"Not until I come from the bedroom. You won't have to wait too long."

I walked down the hall with my bag, laid it across the bed and pulled out my knee-length, dark blue halter dress. I paired it with a pair of gold heels. I put on my gold drop earrings and bracelet, then began to get my hair in order. I then added my makeup for the evening.

I walked out of the bathroom and up the hallway towards the kitchen. I felt it was time for a little liquid courage to ease the nerves. I looked on Anthony's bar and found a bottle of whiskey. I grabbed a glass and poured a shot. I downed it in seconds. It burned a little, but it was just what I needed to calm my nerves. I acted just how I felt; like I haven't had a date in a long time. Just as I was putting his liquor away, Anthony walked up to the living room. He had on a white fitted button up and grey dress slacks. I could smell his cologne before he walked into the room. I felt the fire creep back up between my thighs again, and I tried to keep it contained. His demeanor was mesmerizing. He knew he looked good, and I knew it too.

"Well, I see you've been acquainted with my bar."

"Yes, I have. I'm a little nervous. Figured a shot would calm me down."

"Well, did it do the trick?"

"A little. The way you're looking right now doesn't help though. You look very handsome, Anthony."

"Well you definitely don't look half bad yourself, baby. Come on, let's go before I make us late," he said.

"Don't be nasty."

Anthony led me outside to his car, and we got in and headed to our location for the evening. It was a very nice Mediterranean restaurant, which told me he was actually listening when I told him I had always wanted to try Mediterranean food. It was very small, but from what I could see, very popular. There was a line outside the doors.

Once we got in and were seated, we both ordered drinks

and appetizers. The evening was starting off so well. Once we received our drinks, Anthony asked me a few more serious questions.

"So, I have to ask; how far you see this going between us? I mean, am I worth investing in?"

I took a sip of my wine and took a deep breath, "well, so far, I'm very optimistic about our relationship. I've been having fun and I haven't been this happy in a long time. You make me feel.... different, but in a good way," I said, as I took a sip of wine. "And to answer your question, yes. I feel like I can invest a lot of my time and effort into you; and I hope you feel the same way about me."

"Oh, I do, but you're going to have to expand on...different. In what ways is this different than your relationship with Trey?"

I paused. We hadn't yet approached the topic of my previous relationship with Trey, and the context of it. He knew the basis of why we are divorced, but that's about all I was willing to talk about up until this point. I figured, if we are going to make this serious, it was time to divulge a little more.

"Well, I'll admit, I am much more mature now than I was in my marriage. I've learned a lot of lessons since then. I could sit here and place a lot of blame on Trey, say that he didn't pay me any attention, that he was cheating on me and that is why I retaliated, or even could say that we just fell out of love; but I cannot do that with a clear conscious. The truth is, I handled issues in my marriage inappropriately. I chose to seek comfort and the needs I craved with other men, because I felt like Trey couldn't meet them. If I could go back, I would definitely be more of an adult about things and take the necessary steps to try and fix my marriage, instead of ruining it. My biggest fear is trust. I want you to know I'm different now and I've learned the error of my ways; so you've got nothing to worry about."

"Typically, I don't play this role; but I am not going to sit here and act like I feel like your divorce to Trey didn't start to feel like a blessing in disguise for me. In a weird way, if life wouldn't have taken the paths they took for us, then our paths wouldn't have crossed. I would never have had the opportunity to be with you now, and it's a great feeling for me. I mean, I definitely don't agree with how you chose to handle the issues in your marriage, but at the same time, no one is perfect, and we all deserve second chances. I told you that, and I would never try and hold it against you. It is a part of your past, and I can acknowledge that; however, I am confident that with me, we will have a very successful relationship. All the other shit is in the past and I'm not even thinking about it."

Anthony knew just what to say to make me smile. I could appreciate that he didn't judge what happened in my marriage and was willing to take a chance with me. The waiter came to our table with our food, and to see if we needed anything. I ordered another glass of wine and Trey ordered a whiskey, neat.

"Well Anthony, I'm glad you feel that way, and I'm glad you're willing to not use my past to judge me. I want you to feel comfortable with me, and I also want you to be able to see a future with me."

"So, you see a future with me?" he asked.

I took a minute to sip my drink, "Yes. I don't want to rush too much, but I honestly see me, you and Chelsea being a family one day. So, a girl can dream a bit, I hope."

"Good; so do I," Anthony said, and he proceeded to take a bite of his food. I smiled at him and began eating my food as well. I didn't know what to say. I had no idea that he was that serious about us.

"Did I say something wrong? You went silent on me."

"No! No sweetie, you actually are saying all the right things. It's been a long time since I have heard all the right things being said to me. You're very intentional with your words and I like that."

"Well, I'm at a point now where I don't want to play games. I was beginning to give up on love. But I see now that I have found someone I can enjoy the present with and look towards the future with too. So, I'm glad about that," he said with a smirk.

Anthony had no idea how much ease that gave me. He just made it plain and clear that he is truly falling for who I am now, and not who I was, and that allowed me to let my guard down just a little bit more.

We had a wonderful dinner, we laughed and talked and drank all night long. With every conversation I felt closer and closer to him. I loved how confident he was in telling me just how he saw our future together, and it definitely put me in a good place. On the ride home, I was feeling the buzz and based on our combined alcohol intake, the sexual tension was real between us. As Anthony drove back to his house, I began to rub my hand up and down his thigh. I saw him smirk in the corner of my eye.

"What are you doing, Chante?"

I played dumb, "What do you mean?"

"You know what I mean. You trying to make me pull this car over and do you in the backseat, aren't you?"

"Unless you're into that kind of thing. I can jump in the backseat while you pick a spot to put the car in park."

"As good as that sounds, I'd much rather take you home, lay you across my king-sized bed, where you would be comfortable and fuck you until you can't move."

"Shit. I see what the alcohol does to him," I thought. I was beginning to wonder what I had gotten myself into, because

Anthony sounds like he is going to put me through it, in the best and worst way. But instead of showing doubt, I turned it up a notch to show him that I was just as equally ready for the night's activities as he was.

I continued to run my hand up his thigh until I reached his dick. It was already growing by the minute. Anthony licked his lips and shot me a sexy glance that told me that as soon as we got into his house, it was on.

It took less than a minute for Anthony to plant his lips on mine once we stepped into his house. As soon as he turned the key and I stepped inside, he grabbed my waist and pulled me close into him, so that I could feel his dick against my leg. Our lips never separated as I took off my shoes and helped Anthony unbutton his shirt. I stopped kissing him long enough to take his hand and lead him to his bedroom. There was a lot of heavy breathing, pants of anticipation and excitement. This was possibly the one moment we had both been waiting on in these last couple months more than anything.

Once we got to Anthony's bedroom, he laid me on the bed and began to take my dress off. Luckily for me, I wasn't wearing any panties, so that was one less thing he had to remove. Once he saw my body, he couldn't resist. He couldn't stop kissing me on every part of my body; my neck, my breast, my stomach, each thigh; all the way down to my feet. I was being spoiled with how much time he took to appreciate each and every part of my body.

From my legs, he ventured back up to my thighs. I arched my back and lifted my ass up for easier access to what he wanted. He started slowly, kissing the outer lips, placing small, subtle bites along my inner thigh, licking me from my belly button to my pelvis. He teased and teased until I couldn't take anymore.

"Anthony! Stop playing with me!"

His laugh was mischievous, like a little boy who had just got caught in a game of hide and seek. "I don't know what you're talking about."

He placed another kiss on the innermost part of my thigh, as close to my spot as he could get without actually making contact.

"I can't stand you," I said smiling.

Anthony looked down and proceeded to ease his tongue slowly to part my lips. He licked up and down my opening as I moaned in complete bliss. I prayed his walls weren't thin, but I didn't really give a shit. I didn't intend on being quiet tonight. I let my inner freak out and continued to moan and yell all through his house. I placed my hand on the top of his head and moved it on my demand; guiding him up and down, left and right.

He picked up his intensity and stuck his tongue all the way inside me and moved it back and forth. As he did that, he took his thumb and index finger and rubbed my clit as he licked. He was an animal and I loved every minute of it. He wouldn't stop no matter how many times I tried to push his head away. It felt so good it hurt! Instead of honoring my request to slow down, Anthony's tongue moved faster against my clit. He gripped my legs and pinned them so I couldn't move. He wanted me to feel every sensation, every lick and every suck. I felt everything, until my body went into convulsions from the feeling of passion. I grabbed the sheets and held them until my body ceased to shake. I exhaled in relief.

"Damn."

That's all I could say. And it was only the beginning. I couldn't wait for what else was in store.

Anthony emerged from between my thighs, taking his hand and wiping the wetness from his lips.

"Damn baby. You taste amazing."

"I'm glad you enjoyed yourself. That had to be the best head I've ever gotten."

Our eyes met, and he placed his tongue gently into my mouth, allowing me to savor my flavor as he moved his tongue around. We exchanged in passionate and lengthy kisses, unleashing all the tension that had been pent up in our bodies for months. Anthony did not miss a beat as he proceeded to remove his boxers as I looked on. As he pulled his boxers off, his dick swung out, standing long, erect and ready to please. I was salivating at the thought of finally being able to feel this man inside of me. I sat up and caressed his throbbing manhood with my fingers. I ran my perfectly manicured nails up and down the shaft. Anthony pushed me back onto the bed and grabbed my ankles to pull me closer to the edge of the bed. He lifted my ass up slightly for a better angle, then proceeded to slide his dick inside of me.

With each stroke, I was drifting further and further. This man knew exactly how to please his lover and wasted no time with me. He moved his hips slowly but intensely, making sure to fill me with every inch. I couldn't control my moans and soon I was matching him stroke for stroke.

"Ooooh baby.... yes, YES.....keep going baby.....right there, stay right there."

I couldn't control my body at this point, I was gyrating my hips against his, making sure I received every stroke he was giving me. His speed picked up, and he put my legs up on his shoulders. He was so deep, and as he stared into my eyes, I knew we were both on the way to a happy ending. He pounded me fiercely as he felt the moment arising, "shit baby, I'm about to come!"

I was right there with him, gripping the bed as my pussy pulsated on his dick in ecstasy. He grabbed my thighs and he continued to release himself inside of me. I could feel our bodies both trembling with satisfaction. We looked into each other's eyes, both with looks of satisfaction. He placed soft kisses on my lips, my forehead, my cheeks. I returned with a subtle kiss behind his ear and on his neck.

Anthony was fast asleep, as I laid across his chest, kissing him softly while he slept. There was a sense of euphoria in the atmosphere of his bedroom. Being with Anthony made me realize just how long it had been since I had felt a man's touch and allowed a man to please me the way I deserved. Along with everything else that happened over the course of the evening, this type of loving is something I could get used to on a regular basis.

I woke up the next morning, love drunk from the night before. I was hungover from the passionate love making after dinner, and the middle-of-the-night quickie around 3am. Anthony was lying next to me, with his arm across my stomach. His finger was tracing an outline around my body's silhouette.

"You're awake."

"Yes; I've been waiting on you."

"What do you mean?"

"I need you. I haven't been able to get last night, and this morning off my mind. Plus, I woke up with this," Anthony pulled the comforter off of him, to expose his obviously hard manhood.

"Well, someone is happy to see me this morning."

Anthony took his hand and placed two fingers inside of me.

"Very happy."

I grabbed the back of his neck and pulled him closer, kissing him. The second his lips met mine; I was hot and ready. He wrapped his arms around me and flipped me on top of him. I mounted his dick and began to ride him slowly. Our erotic moans filled the morning air.

"Damn baby, this feels so good.."

I jumped up and down on his dick. He couldn't get enough of it. By the looks on his face, I would say I was doing a damn good job at morning sex, so I decided to show off. I reversed on him and rode him in a reverse cowgirl position. Anthony grabbed ahold of my ass and gripped it as he bounced me up and down on his dick. I could feel him grip my hips tighter, which meant he was getting into it. He moved my body rapidly, trying to control when and how he came. I tried to manipulate the situation, but he was too strong. He worked me just as good as I worked him. In unison, we both arrived at our second orgasm of the morning. It was the best start to the day that I could have imagined. I rolled over onto my stomach and let him leave a trail of kisses down my spine. I knew if this was what our weekends together would be like, I would never want to leave to go home.

About an hour later, I woke up again from the nap I had taken after our morning sex. I realized Anthony wasn't in bed with me when I woke up. I sat straight up in the bed and saw a t-shirt on the edge of his bed. I decided to throw it on and head to the living room to see if he was there.

I walked towards his bathroom and then out to his living room. It was clear that he had went somewhere, his keys were not on the dining room table where he left them last night. I admitted to myself that I wouldn't be a woman if I didn't do a little snooping around his place while I had the chance. My womanly senses were telling me to check and make sure there were no mystery pictures of a second family tucked in a nightstand drawer, or panties in the couch cushions from his random one-night stands when I wasn't here. Being in a long-distance relationship is hard, and I had to admit that I had some insecurities about whether or not he was completely faithful. I mean, looking at him, I would have to guess that women commonly throw themselves at him often. I tried to shake all of that out of my mind and decided against snooping through the drawers and couch cushions. Sometimes, going to look for something will cause you to find the things you don't want; and right now, I was happy and didn't want to mess up that feeling. I decided to pour a glass of water, and step outside onto his porch.

The LA breeze hit my skin and it felt amazing, like it could and would take my breath away. It was the perfect summer morning. The sun was shining just like in movies. I felt like this was the weather 365 days a year. I looked out and could see mountains in the distance. It was like a postcard; I was in a real-life postcard. Part of me did feel like I could pick up my entire life and move here just for the beautiful weather alone. I didn't know if I could do that to Chelsea, and Trey would have a fit if he wasn't close to her. Suddenly, I felt a slight twinge of regret, *"Why am I thinking about him and what he wants?"*

Standing on Anthony's patio allowed me to really think. I have made more than willing accommodations to my life so that Trey can also be able to continue to be a part of Chelsea's life; however, I feel like I may be hindering myself as well. I could be losing out on a great man for the sake of a very big distance, and nothing says I cannot move to be closer to him, if we truly have a chance. I thought about the conversation that Anthony and I had at dinner, and him wanting me and Chelsea to be in his life. If that is truly the case, then I would be willing to make that sacrifice for love. And I think I was falling for Anthony Bishop.

I heard the front door unlock and open. Anthony came in the door with breakfast in a bag and coffee in his hand. He saw me on the patio and walked over to me.

"I figured you would be hungry after all that energy you gave out this morning." He kissed me softly on the cheek.

"And you are correct. What'd you get?"

Anthony sat down at his patio table and pulled out a box with two pancakes, turkey bacon, scrambled egg whites and smoked salmon.

"This looks great baby"

"I hope you enjoy it. It's from one of the places I go on my way to work. I go there at least three times a week. They've got the best pancakes."

We both sipped our coffee and ate our meal. Famine had taken over our bodies and we had not even realized it.

I was so focused on eating, that I barely saw Anthony look up at me and ask, "so, when will I get to finally meet Chelsea?"

"Do you think you are ready for that?"

"I think so. It's not like I am afraid of you having a child or anything. What I do know is that if I know this is going to be serious, then I'm ready to start getting to know her."

"Ok. Well, I guess the next time we see each other it will be your turn to come to me, so you can meet her then. We can set up a date with her so you guys can get to know each other."

Anthony leaned over and kissed Chante, "I can't wait."

Anthony told me to shower and get dressed after I ate, because he had a load of sight-seeing for us to do that day. He still kept it very discreet on what we did, but I still obliged and took a shower and got dressed.

We were heading into downtown LA, to do some shopping and walk around, just so I could get a taste of Los Angeles. Most of what I see is the inside of hotels, bookstores and airports; so, I never got to really experience what LA is like. Anthony let me do whatever it was that I wanted. He walked around as I shopped like I had a million dollars to blow. He saw me eyeing a few things, and he managed to convince me to let him buy me a few things.

He was not lying when he said he wanted to spoil me. He took me to some bookstores; including the one we reunited in that sparked our relationship. Later that evening, he drove me to Hollywood Boulevard to see the Walk of Fame. When we were finally on the way back to his place, I was grinning from ear to ear. It felt good to be on vacation, and especially to be spending my time with Anthony.

That night, we stayed in and decided to watch some movies, and I decided to pull out a lingerie piece that I bought for the occasion. Needless to say, we didn't even get through one movie before he picked me up and carried me back to the bedroom.   On the last day of my trip to LA, I was more emotional that I didn't want it to end. Everything had been so perfect and easy. Anthony was the perfect gentleman throughout the entire trip, and it was definitely nice to be catered to and courted for a change. You would have thought that we had been dating for years, by the way we eased into being in each other's company. Anthony was driving me to the airport; our hands interlocked and lying on my left thigh. Every now and then he would sneak a peek at me as I looked out of the window, taking in the last few moments of LA I would have for a while.

"So, be honest with me; did you enjoy yourself?"

I turned back to him and smiled, "I don't even want to leave. You made this such a great trip for me."

I could see Anthony smiling as he continued to watch the road, "I'm really glad to hear that. I wanted to make sure I included all the different things you have told me you wanted to do here. I was hoping I was making a good impression for you."

"You outdid yourself, babe. I cannot wait to come back and do it all over again."

He glanced in my direction, but not so much that would take his eyes off the road, "do you know when that might be, by chance?"

I hesitated for a moment; not because I didn't want to, but because I truly hadn't thought about it.

"I'm not sure yet. I'm sure I have a ton of work I need to do back at the office. But once I get all that sorted out, I will be booking my next flight to California, after you come see me of course."

Anthony glanced at me, "you mean *I* will be booking your next flight."

"Anthony, I cannot continue to allow you to purchase my plane tickets out here. It's just too much."

"Listen, if I want you to come out to see me, then I will spare no expense to get you here. It's really no problem, and I look at it as a way to spoil you a bit. So, if you don't mind, please let me have my moments to treat you like a queen, ok?"

I sat back and shut my mouth. I wasn't going to argue or debate over it. It was clear that he wanted to do nice things for me, so I was not going to stop him. It was hard, because I had easily adapted into the independent single woman and mother mode; however, if Anthony wanted me to ease up a bit and let him take control, I wasn't going to stand in his way.

We finally arrived to the airport. I almost didn't want to leave his side. He got my bags out of the car and walked them up to the check-in counter for me. After I was all checked in, I gave him the longest hug and kiss ever. We looked into each other's eyes, and he almost convinced me to stay with just the look on his face.

"Don't get me all in love with you, just for you to ghost me when you get back to DC," he said in between kisses.

"I would never do that. I don't know what you did to me, Anthony; but I'm all into you."

"Me too, babe. Me too."

I gave him one final kiss and promised him a text when I got home.

"I love you," I said. It just came out before I could even stop it, but I wasn't even mad. He got me, and I didn't want to be anywhere else but with him.

"I love you too, Chante. And I'm not saying it just because you said it," he said.

I smiled and went towards my gate.

While I sat at the gate, I pulled out my phone to shoot a text to Nia. I had to tell someone what I had just done, and what I had gotten myself into.

"Girl, I think I'm in love."

TEN

After four long blissful days on the west coast, I was finally back home in DC and ready to see my baby girl. I got back from the airport and had an Uber take me to Nia's house, where Chelsea was, and I knew she would want to know all the details of my trip. I text Anthony once I touched down to let him know I made it safely back home, and to thank him for the wonderful weekend.

"It was my pleasure babe. Anything and more for you," he replied.

I was already counting the days until we would see each other again, which would be in about a month. We decided that I would finally let Chelsea meet Anthony, now that we both agreed that we were pretty serious with each other. Anthony even said that he would do so much as to get a hotel for those two days so that it wouldn't be awkward with him staying overnight while Chelsea was there. He was going about the situation like a true gentleman and I appreciate him so much for this. I knew this would be something new for Chelsea, so every bit helps.

My Uber pulled up to Nia's brownstone, and I thanked the man and got out. I grabbed my bags from the trunk and walked up to her door. I didn't even knock before the door flew open and Chelsea came out with her arms wide to hug the life out of me.

"Mommy! Mommy! I missed you!"

"I missed you too, princess! Were you good for auntie Nia?"

She nodded.

"Good. I brought you something from my trip, but I will let you open it when we get home."

Chelsea jumped around like she had hit the lottery. She ran back in the house to let Mariya know that she had a surprise waiting for her and they continued to laugh and play. I looked at Nia and gave her a big hug.

"Thank you for keeping Chelsea for me, I really appreciate it girl!"

"Now you know it was no problem. We had a ball at the house. I also took them out for frozen yogurt yesterday. Chelsea says I'm the best auntie ever!"

We both laughed as I brought my bags into the house.

"So, I need details. All the details. How was he? What all did y'all do? Did y'all even leave his apartment with your nasty asses?"

I laughed at all of her questions. "First of all, he was great. We did a little bit of everything; dinner, sight-seeing, hanging out binge watching horrible Netflix shows. We were an actual couple. So, to answer your other question, we left the house; however, once we got back, we spent a lot of time in the bed, if you know what I mean."

"Y'all are NAS-TY!"

"We were simply making up for the times that we are not together. This should definitely hold me over until he comes down in about a month."

"So, he's coming here next? That should be great! Will I get to see this man in person?"

"Yes, I'll make sure you get to see him. He's actually wants to meet Chelsea. I think I'll be ready. I just have to get her ready."

Nia looked at me assuredly, "I'm sure she will be. I think Chelsea is old enough to know that her mama gotta have a life too. And from what it sounds like, Anthony sounds like the perfect gentleman so I'm sure he will be on his best behavior."

"You're right. I don't have anything to worry about."

Talking to Nia definitely gave me more reassurance that I was making the right choice in allowing Anthony to go ahead and meet Chelsea. I think after the talks about how much our relationship was evolving, I think it was time to at least allow her to know that her mom was involved and happy with someone else; especially if Anthony has the potential to be her stepfather.

Later that night, after Chelsea and I got home, I was preparing to put her to bed when I took a deep breath and asked her the question that has been burning in my mind.

"Hey sweetie, mommy has a question."

"Yes mommy." She looked up at me with the most innocent eyes you could ever see.

"So, in a few weeks, mommy will have a friend come and visit that she wants you to meet. Someone that is really special to me."

"Is it a friend like auntie Nia?"

"Well, no. It's a man friend. Mommy has a new man friend that she would like you to meet, because she really likes him and wants you to know him."

I paused for her reaction. I knew she was only five, but I never knew what could be going through that intelligent little mind she has.

"Ok mommy! Do I get a new dress? I want to have new pretty clothes when I meet him so he will like me too."

I smiled, "honey, I'm sure he will like you in any clothes you wear; but if it will help you make a good impression, we will go shopping for a new dress."

"Ok!"

With that, she kissed me on the nose, and snuggled down into her blanket. I think she was happier about the thought of getting something new. I think her mission in life is to spend all my money. But, if it helped with smoothing over the introduction of a new man in our lives, I would buy whatever it took.

Once I got Chelsea to sleep, I called Anthony. He would have been just leaving the gym when I called.

"Hello beautiful."

"Hey sweetie. How was your workout?"

"Hard. I wasn't really feeling it today, but I still got through it."

"Aww babe. Well, I'm glad you got through it."

"Truth is, I would have traded for a different type of workout, with you in my bed."

"That doesn't sound like a bad way to burn calories."

He laughed, "I'm sure talking nasty to me on the phone is not what you called for. What's up baby?"

"I was going to tell you that I told Chelsea that she would be meeting you. She wants to buy a new dress so she will make the best first impression."

"She is adorable. In that case, I better go shopping for a new outfit myself. I don't want her to show out on me; even though I'm sure she will upstage me in anything she has on."

"Well do your best, because I don't want to see you looking

anything less than the sexiest man on the planet."

"Always for you babe."

"I'll talk to you a little later, once you have gotten home and settled, ok?"

"Sounds good baby. Love you."

"Love you too."

I hung up the phone and feeling good about what we had planned. Everything was falling into place for me and I couldn't have been happier. I guess next weekend was going to be a shopping weekend for Chelsea and I, because we have some bomb outfits to pick out for when Anthony comes to DC.

The next weekend came, and Chelsea and I were having our best girls' day, shopping for our new outfits for when Anthony came. Even at her young, tender age of five, she wanted to make a good first impression and was very meticulous when it came to choosing an outfit. We went into at least four different stores, and finally decided on a black and white sunflower dress. We found a matching bow to match, and I would make sure her hair was done perfectly to accommodate it. Meanwhile, I found a complimenting yellow dress to wear to dinner that night. All while we were shopping, Anthony was texting me while he was at work, asking what and how our day was going.

"Are you going to show me what you bought for me?"

"Nope," I text back, *"no sneak peeks. Not even Chelsea's."*

"Aww man. I guess I'll have to stay in suspense 😊*"*

Anthony was going to be in for a treat when he saw us for dinner. I was counting down until he arrived; which was still a few weeks away. Due to a work assignment, he had to schedule his trip a week and a half further out than we had planned, but it was ok. I knew Chelsea would like him, but I was very apprehensive about how she would take another man being in her life that wasn't her father. I hoped it would go over well. I continued to check in with her and answer any questions she had, but so far, it didn't seem like she was totally against it.

ELEVEN

It was early on a Saturday morning, and I was knee deep into cleaning mode. I tried to get an early start on it since Chelsea was fast asleep in her room. I had my playlist going, and I was bouncing through my apartment feeling good. I abruptly stopped when my phone rang through my Bluetooth speaker. It was my mom.

"Hello?"

"Hey baby! How are you doing?"

"Hey mama. I'm good, just cleaning up the house a bit. What are you doing up this early?"

"I'm getting ready to go shopping. You know I like to get to the grocery store early so I can get in and beat the crowds. I hate that shit."

I laughed, "I do know that."

"So, what's been up with you lately, child? How are things going at work?"

"They're good so far. I actually am doing a writer call later this month and you know my book is set to go to the publisher in a few weeks."

"Sounds like hard work. But I know you can handle it. I can't wait for my advance copy of this new one; since you wouldn't give anyone any hints on what it was about."

I rolled my eyes as if she could see me, "mama now you know you can't get all the details. Plus, you run your damn mouth to everyone. The plot would've been all over Facebook if I told you!"

"Hey, you watch your mouth girl. I would have kept it a secret!"

"Yea yea mom. I got you."

"Anyways, when are you going to get you a decent man?" She wasted no time getting into my business.

I smirked a little bit. Just the thought of Anthony made me giggle like a little schoolgirl.

"Well, there is someone I'm seeing at the moment."

"Really?! Who?" she asked. She was so nosey it wasn't even funny.

"His name is Anthony. I've known him since college. We recently connected when I went on my tour stop in LA. Since then, we've been talking and spending some time together. He flew me out to LA a few weeks ago."

I wasn't even going to tell her that I was in love. I wasn't ready to hear her 'don't jump out of love and in love so quickly' speech. She still thinks there is a chance I'm still in love with Trey; even though I have told her constantly that I do love Trey, but I am not in love with him anymore.

"Ohhhhhh! Well ok then girl! Sounds like someone's been finding a way to keep you warm."

"Mama, he can't keep me warm at night. We live on two different coasts."

"Well if you went all the way to LA to see him again, I'm sure y'all did something nasty."

I was officially done with the conversation when she said that, "ok ma, I gotta go. You're trippin' now."

"Oh fine. I guess we'll talk more about him later. Don't think I won't forget to bring this up the next time you call me because I need the details."

We exchanged 'I love you's' and hung up the phone. At least at this point, my mother knows as well. Even though she doesn't know I've dropped the L word, she knows enough to know that I am definitely smitten.

After that, my Saturday was pretty productive. I cleaned the house, took Chelsea to the park. While we were there, I took some pictures of her, since it had been a long time. I sent them to Trey because I try to send him updated pictures. One time, Liyah tried to get pissy; saying I didn't send her any pictures and she would still want some. I politely told her that she can get them from Trey if she really wanted them, but the last time I checked, she did not want me 'texting her fuckin phone'. She quickly shut up and stopped texting me. She makes it more and more difficult to co-parent with Trey every time she attempts to get on my nerves.

Later on that night, I was talking to Nia, since it had been a couple days since we spoke. She was telling me about this new girl she had started to talk to. She said, "I don't think it's love yet, but she is fine as hell. I met her in Atlanta when I did a shoot there. It was right before I met you actually, so it's still kind of fresh and new."

"That's what's up Nia! I hope things evolve into something more serious. You deserve a good relationship as well."

"Yea, but don't rush me. I don't fall in love too quickly, but she might actually have me thinking about an actual relationship."

"I'll have to meet her then."

"You'll have your moment, Tae," she said, laughing. "But enough about me and my little situationship, let's talk about how you and Anthony are about to get married."

"Oh shut the hell up, Nia!" I said as I burst out in laughter, "I am NOT getting married right now. But I did fall pretty hard pretty fast."

"You did, but I'm not mad at you, girl. Seems like you both are really into one another. Who knows where this will end up."

"Yea I hope so. I really like him, Nia. Like really like him. I didn't think I would fall for him like this, but he is perfect for me. And he's fine as hell. He's the ultimate package."

"Yep, you're definitely in love with him. But I support it, girl. Get yours!"

We talked for a little longer and then Anthony called, so I talked to him for a while. We were nearing the countdown to his arrival in DC, and we were both pretty excited. I wasn't sure what to expect, but I knew we would have fun. I couldn't wait for him to finally get here.

So, the day was finally here; Anthony was finally coming to meet me here in DC. I woke up that morning earlier than expected; which I attributed to the nerves of him coming. I had no doubts that this weekend would be a great one, but I still got butterflies every time I was preparing to see him face to face. I decided that instead of lying in bed and wallowing in my anxiety, I got up, put on some music and prepared my day for the arrival of the love of my life.

About an hour later, Chelsea woke up and came into my room. I was cleaning my bathroom and had just changed the sheets on my bed when she came running in.

"Morning mommy!"

"Good morning, princess. How did you sleep?"

"Good. Is Mr. Anthony coming today?"

"Yes; he will be here in about two hours. I am going to let you go see auntie Nia and Mariya for the night, and then I will come pick you up for breakfast, ok?"

I decided that for the first night that Anthony was here, I would let Chelsea stay with Nia, and then she can meet him the next day. There was some necessary alone time that Anthony and I would need, and I didn't want my daughter in the next room while I was getting my back blown out by my boyfriend.

"Ok. Let me go get ready." Chelsea then scurried off to her bedroom to get dressed and brush her teeth.

I decided to take Chelsea's advice and begin getting myself freshened up to drop her off and head to the airport. I hopped in the shower and blasted the music as loud as it could go. I was in a great mood and ready to see my man. I washed up, did my hair and slid on a pair of jeans and a sweatshirt. I pulled my hair back into a ponytail and threw on my favorite pair of Nike Air Max. I took a look at myself in the mirror, took a deep breath and smiled, "My baby's coming to town."

I peeked in on Chelsea to make sure she was ready. She had on her sunglasses, a red T-shirt, jacket and leggings. She had packed her own overnight bag, which I checked, because I was sure that all she had in her bag was toys. I went to her closet, grabbed an outfit and pajamas and threw them in the bag. All of the other things she needed were already there. She looked up at me and smiled, "I'm ready!"

"Now that mommy has packed you some clothes, yes; you are ready," I said with a laugh.

I drove to take Chelsea to Nia's house, then made my way to the airport to wait on Anthony. Based on my timing, I should make it about fifteen minutes before the time he said his plane would land. That would give me just enough time to park and go to his gate.

As I was walking into the airport, my phone buzzed. It was Anthony.

"Hey babe. I'm here. Where are you?"

"Walking up to the airport now. Just parked the car. I will meet you at baggage claim."

I picked up the pace in my walk so that I could meet him there. I walked through the airport, looking at all the baggage claim lines to see where I needed to meet Anthony. I found his flight and stood there waiting on him. I hadn't seen anyone coming off flights yet, so I took a seat, and scrolled aimlessly through work emails and social media. I was so engrossed in an email that I received from one of my writers, begging for an extension, that I didn't even see Anthony walk up in front of me. I felt a presence over my head, so I looked up, and the most handsome face and smile was looking back at me.

I jumped up out of my chair and hugged him as tight as possible. Feeling his arms around me felt just as good as the first time we saw each other a couple months ago.

Anthony wasted no time, he looked at me and gave me a deep, long and passionate kiss. I looked at him and smiled. These days I could never stop smiling whenever I was near him. We both just stood there, embraced, taking in the idea of physically being present with one another.

"I've missed you," I said staring him straight in his eyes.

"Likewise."

"I doubt you've missed me as much as I've missed you."

"I will prove it to you, in due time. For now, let's get my bag and get out of here."

I kissed him on the lips and walked with him towards the baggage claim to wait for his bag. Once we saw it come across the belt, he grabbed it and we were on our way. When we got to the car, he insisted that he drove us back to my place.

"Babe, you just got off a long flight, I can drive you around."

"The gentleman nature in me won't allow it. To the passenger side you go, ma'am."

I reluctantly obliged him and navigated our way out of the parking deck at the airport, and towards my apartment.

In about 20 minutes, we made it to my apartment. We had a little small talk during the drive, mostly Anthony complaining about the traffic and how it's worse that LA traffic. I obviously disagreed with him, but he did not want to hear it. We pulled up and he put the car in park.

"Well, we're here."

"Yep. You finally get to see my place. I'll admit I had to make sure I cleaned up before you came. I was running around like a mad woman this morning."

"I'm sure it wasn't that bad. You don't even carry yourself like that type of woman. I'm sure you didn't have to do much cleaning to this place."

Anthony hopped out of the car and grabbed his suitcase from the trunk. I got out and walked to the door and put my key in. When Anthony walked in, he smiled.

"Your place is nice, babe! Definitely nicer than mine."

I smiled as I took his bag and placed it in my bedroom.

"Make yourself at home. If you're anything like me, you

want a drink after a flight. My bar is next to the kitchen. I got your favorite bottle of cognac."

He walked over to my bar and smiled, "thanks babe."

I walked back into the living room, and Anthony had definitely made himself at home. He had kicked off his shoes, poured a drink and had the TV on ESPN. I feel like that was all he watched.

"My TV hasn't gotten much action on that channel since the last time we FaceTime'd and I watched it with you."

"Really? Well sit down and let's catch the highlights of these games."

I smirked at him while I poured myself a drink, "that's not really what I had in mind."

Anthony looked over at me, and saw me as I sipped my drink slowly. He downed the remainder of his drink, turned the TV off and walked towards me.

"I guess this means we have some business to discuss in the bedroom."

I finished my drink, took off my shirt, exposing my black laced bra, "yes, we definitely do."

Anthony picked me up and began kissing me as he carried me to my bedroom. I was kissing him all over his neck and shoulders as he carried me.

When we got to the bedroom, it was on. Clothes were flying, bodies were clashing and soon we were in between my freshly washed linen sheets, making enough noise for the neighbors to hear our moans. For the first time Anthony had the opportunity to christen the sheets on my bed, he did not disappoint; and I could tell he had wanted this just as bad as I did.

After about two hours of pleasure-filled bliss, there we were, lying in bed, eating ice cream and watching all the shows I had neglected to watch on my DVR throughout the week. I was sitting up in the bed, and Anthony's head was in my lap as he caressed my thigh. He didn't say much, outside of comments that only a man would say about the "ratchet TV" I liked to watch.

"I still don't see how you can watch all this crazy shit. This is some pure foolishness."

"It is my dose of entertainment outside of my crazy real life. I enjoy it. You don't have to, but just know that this is my favorite pastime and if you are going to be spending time here, you have to accept it."

"If you enjoy it, then I'll tolerate it. I could lay in bed with you all day and all night long; watching you eat your fat kid snacks and yell at the TV."

We both laughed. I fed him spoonful's of ice cream in between mine until my small carton was gone. After that, I sunk down under my duvet comforter and Anthony readjusted so that I could lay my head on his chest. I ran my fingertips across his chest as I lay there. It was something about the environment; him lying in my bed, being in the presence of the man I loved, but I started to feel the heat once again. I continued to trace a trail across his chest and abs, until my hands found his dick. I rubbed it until I felt him rise to attention.

"Oh, so this is what you doing now?"

"I can't help it; I want what I want. And by your reaction, I can tell that you want it too."

"I guess you could say that."

Anthony rolled me over onto my back and took two fingers and slid them into my sweet spot. I moaned in delight as he used his fingers to get me good and ready for what was next to come. He kissed me as he grabbed me by my neck and pulled me closer up to him. I wrapped my arms around his neck and continued to kiss him. He proceeded to enter me slow and gentle. It felt so damn good. I pulled his body closer to mine with every thrust of his hips. The intensity in our love making was unmatched. I had never felt this way about any man that I had been with previously. There was a certain chemistry between us that mixed with our passion to make this moment better every time.

Anthony continued to move in a rhythm of love as he pulled in and out. He turned me over onto my stomach and began to stroke me from behind. He positioned me over the side of my bed and slide back in where he rightfully belonged. He held my breast in his hands and played with my nipples. I gripped my sheets and began to ride him back. With every thrust I pushed myself back onto him with the same level of energy. Anthony took one hand and grabbed my hair and pulled me into him while he kissed me up and down my spine. There was so much licking, sucking, grabbing and pulling that I couldn't keep up. I was lost in the lust of it all. Whoever made the phrase "absence makes the heart grow fonder", must have not realized that it makes a few other things grow fonder as well.

TWELVE

The next morning, Anthony was still asleep when I woke up. I could imagine he was hungover, which was apparent from the two bottles of wine on my nightstand on top of the alcohol we drank last night. He had to be exhausted, with the flight and dirty sex we had all night. I looked over at the clock, and it read 6:30am. I decided to get out of bed and make breakfast for the both of us since we had a long day ahead. Today, I planned on taking Anthony into the heart of DC with Chelsea to see different museums, because he was into that type of thing. I remember him going on and on about how he has always wanted to get up close and personal with some of the monuments and see at least one museum. I figured it would be the perfect day, since I haven't gotten to tour much of DC, and it would be a great experience for everyone to have.

I slipped from under Anthony's arm and out of bed without him making a move. I grabbed his t-shirt at the end of the bed and went into the kitchen and pulled out all the ingredients I needed to make French toast, smoked salmon, eggs, and fruit. I put on some music and got into my zone. It was a perfect Saturday morning; the sun was just barely peeking through the curtain in my living room. I tried not to make too much noise, as to not disturb Anthony. I wanted to make sure everything was perfect, as I sang along to the music, mixing, baking and prepping our meal.

A few minutes later, I could hear my bathroom door close. Anthony was awake. I went into the refrigerator and grabbed the orange juice and poured him a glass. When he came around the corner to the kitchen, he looked at me. I looked up at him and smiled, with a ready-made glass of orange juice in my hand

"Good morning," he said. His voice was a sexy sort of raspy since he had just woke up.

I walked over to him, and kissed him gently, "good morning babe. How did you sleep?"

"Great. You sure do know how to get a man a good night's rest," he said smirking at me and kissing me on my forehead.

"I do my best. Did you enjoy yourself?"

"Did I? I'm hoping there's more where that came from."

"If you play your cards right, it will be."

Anthony walked towards the table, drinking his juice. "So, what's on the menu baby? And what do you have planned for me today?"

I put the finishing touches on our plates and walked over to the table to join him.

"Well, after breakfast, we're going to get ready and go get Chelsea. Then we are going to head to DC for a day full of adventure."

Anthony's face seemed to light up at the statement as he took a big bite of his French toast, "adventure huh? Well I hope it's a fun one. And I cannot wait to meet Chelsea. I hope she likes me."

"I'm sure she will love you."

We continued to eat breakfast and after that, I shot Nia a quick text letting her know to have Chelsea ready within the next hour and then jumped in the shower to get ready. While I was in the shower, I heard the bathroom door open and close. I looked outside the shower curtain and saw Anthony standing there, naked.

"What are you doing?" I asked.

"I figured we could save water and shower together."

"By the looks of things, it looks like you want to do more than just shower."

Anthony smirked, and walked towards the shower. He pulled the curtain back, stepped in and placed his hands on my shoulders. He kissed my neck from behind so, I took a tiny step back, placing my ass against his dick, that was already rock hard. He continued to kiss me from one side of my back to the other. I turned to him and began kissing his chest. We both made the decision that we would have to be a few minutes late, there was something that decided to pop up.

On the ride to Nia's house, I was very nervous. I kept thinking of every way possible that this first introduction between Chelsea and Anthony. As I was driving, Anthony could sense my nervousness and asked, "what's wrong, babe?"

"Just thinking. I hope Chelsea likes you as much as I do. I haven't introduced her to a man since Trey and I divorced. I don't know what to expect."

"I'm sure Chelsea is very mature for her age and will be fine. I hope she likes me too."

"Are you nervous?"

"Who wouldn't be? First time I am meeting my girlfriend's most important person in her life right now. I am more nervous than you think."

Knowing that he was a little nervous about their meeting, somehow put me at ease. It let me know that he was really serious about being a part of Chelsea's life and doesn't want to mess things up. He knows that Chelsea is a big part of my life, and if she is not fond of him, then we could never have a relationship.

We pulled up to Nia's house, preparing to see Chelsea. I turned the car off and grabbed Anthony's hand.

"Well, here we go. Ready?"

"Ready."

I got out of the car and ran up to Nia's front door. Anthony trailed behind me as I waited at the door. I hear Chelsea run to the door and open it.

"Mommy! I missed you," Chelsea said as she squeezed my legs. I thought she would never let go.

"I missed you too sweetie. Look, there is someone I want you to meet."

Chelsea peeked around my legs to see Anthony standing behind me, with a smile on his face.

"Hello Chelsea. I'm Anthony."

"Hi, Mr. Anthony. I'm Chelsea." Chelsea ran over to Anthony and shook his hand. She smiled at him, almost as a welcome into her life.

Anthony knelt down in front of Chelsea, "Are you ready for a day full of adventures?"

"Yes!" she yelled, with her eyes lighting up at the thought of everything she could get into today.

I watched their interaction in awe. So far, everything had been going great. I didn't want there to be any awkwardness between them, and so far, it looks like they were doing ok.

I told both Anthony and Chelsea to come inside with me, while I told Nia that we were leaving. Nia was walking back from Mariya's room, putting her down for her nap.

"Well, Anthony Bishop. I've heard so many things about

you! I'm Nia, Chante's best friend and Chelsea's play auntie," she said jokingly.

Anthony chuckled, "Hey Nia. I have heard good things about you as well. I hope what you have heard isn't more bad things than good."

"Oh trust me, Chante only tells me the *good* things." Nia looked over at me and winked.

I shot her a side eye and laughed, "*ANYWAYS*, yes Anthony, this is the Nia I have told you about so many times on the phone. She has been a Godsend ever since I have been in DC. And sometimes, she gets on my nerves a bit."

"Well, I'm very glad to meet you Nia. We're going to have to get together and you'll have to tell me some of the deep, dark, dirty secrets about Chante."

"I got you. I'll tell you whatever you need to know," she said.

I decided it was time for me to interject, "Ok, now that we got all of that out of the way, it's time to go. We're going to be late."

"You're right baby. I'm ready when you are."

I grabbed Chelsea's overnight bag and gave Nia a hug, "thank you love for watching her last night."

"No problem, girl. She was no problem at all," Nia said. She pulled me closer and whispered in my ear, "he's a keeper Chante, I can tell. If you need me to watch Chelsea another night, just say the word...cuz he is fine."

I laughed, "I'll let you know."

We all walked out to the car, headed to our adventures. Anthony helped Chelsea into the car, and then ran over to open the door for me.

Once he got in the car, I finally decided to reveal our plans for the day, "so, I know you always mentioned how you love going to museums and all, so I figured we can tour the Smithsonian's today. How's that sound?"

Anthony smiled, "sounds great! I didn't even think you remembered that. I guess you have been listening to me."

"Of course, I was. I figured since Chelsea hasn't seen them either, this would be a perfect experience for you both."

"Well, let's go then! I'm excited" Anthony said. He leaned over and gave me a small kiss on the cheek. He was being on his best behavior in front of Chelsea.

I looked behind me in my rearview mirror, "Chels, you ready to go to the museums?"

"YES!!" she said with a big grin on her face.

I put my car in drive and we went on our way towards DC.

THIRTEEN

The day spent in DC was great. Once we got there and parked, Anthony wasted no time going full tourist mode downtown. He enjoyed every minute of it. He was also perfect with Chelsea. She took to him very easily, and soon they were walking, running and holding hands down the sidewalk, while I walked behind them just watching the two interact. Anthony was a natural with children. He was definitely having fun and wanted to make sure Chelsea was too. They held hands as we walked through the museums and all-around downtown to see the monuments. When she got tired, he carried her on his shoulders so she could be tall enough to see everything. She had so much joy and happiness on her face, I wished the day wouldn't end.

At the end of the day, we all stopped to get ice cream, which Anthony paid for. We sat down at one of the parks, while Chelsea ran and played under the trees.

"So, it looks like you guys are having a lot of fun," I said as I ate a scoop of ice cream.

"Tons! She is awesome, Chante. You have raised a beautiful, intelligent and sweet little girl. She is pretty cool."

"I'm glad you guys are besties now," I said laughing, "I was nervous at first, but just watching you guys today let me know that she is comfortable around you and likes you."

"I hope so. I've been pulling out all of my good 'impress your girlfriends' six-year-old daughter' moves."

I laughed, "well they look like they are working out quite nicely. She likes you; I can tell. Chelsea is pretty clear on her actions when she doesn't like someone, and it looks like she definitely likes you."

Anthony looked on while Chelsea played, "yea, I hope she does."

We both looked on as Chelsea ran around and smiled at us as she played. I was so glad that Chelsea had given her unofficial stamp of approval on Anthony. It was further confirmation that there is hope for me despite my past.

Once the sun started to go down, Anthony and I decided we would go back to my place and get ready for dinner. Anthony decided to tell Chelsea and see how she would like it.

"So, Chelsea, I know you have spent a long day with me; did you have fun?"

"Uh huh" Chelsea said as she was playing on her phone.

"Well, I have one more thing for us to do today. I wanted to take you and your mommy out to eat at a very nice restaurant. Would you like that?"

"Is there dessert at the restaurant?"

I interjected, "Chelsea, you cannot have any dessert if you don't eat your food at the restaurant."

"Ok....Mr. Anthony, is there good food at this restaurant because I really want dessert. I have to find something that I like to eat."

Anthony laughed, "yes, sweetie. There is some really good food here. I promise I will help you find something to eat that you're sure to like, then you can have the biggest dessert; my treat."

"Yay!"

Once we all got to my house, Chelsea ran off to her room to

get ready for her dinner. I followed behind her and told Anthony he could get ready in my room, and when I was done with Chelsea, I would get ready.

"Is there anything you need me to do while you get her ready?" he asked.

"No, baby. I'm good. Thank you." I said smiling.

I was having the best day ever at this point. I went into Chelsea's room to help her get showered and changed. I decided now would be the best time to pick her brain about Anthony.

"So, Chels, how did you enjoy the day with Mr. Anthony?"

"It was super fun mommy. Is Mr. Anthony going to be my new daddy?"

I looked at her, stunned, "well, that's not really something you need to worry about right now sweetheart. But, mommy does like Mr. Anthony a lot, so you will be seeing him a lot more often."

"Well, that's good mommy, because I like him. He was really nice to me and wants to buy me dessert after dinner. He could be my new daddy if you wanted. I like him."

I gave Chelsea a kiss on the forehead and continued helping her get ready for the evening. With that, I was officially at ease with Chelsea getting to know Anthony. That night, we had the most wonderful evening at dinner. Anthony was the perfect gentleman. He pulled out our chairs, ordered our food, and as promised, got Chelsea the biggest dessert on the menu. She and Anthony shared it. It was the perfect day. I was happy that they both had a lot of fun. On the ride home, Chelsea was asleep from a dessert coma. Anthony drove the way home while I sat on the passenger side.

"I hope you had fun today, Chante, because I did. We felt like the perfect little family."

"It did, didn't it?"

"Yea. I could definitely get used to that feeling, if you don't mind getting used to it."

"I don't think that is something I would hate, babe. I'm glad you had fun. And by the way Chelsea is snoring, she had fun as well."

When we got home, Anthony carried Chelsea into her room and laid her on her bed, so she could go to sleep. I changed her into her pajamas, while Anthony went and got a little more comfortable. I told him to pull out a bottle of wine that we could share, since we were nowhere near tired at that point.

When I got into my room, I went into the bathroom and changed into my long silk robe. I didn't expect anything to happen tonight while Chelsea was in the house, but I still wanted to set a very intimate mood. I walked back out to the living room, and Anthony had the TV on SportsCenter. He had opened the bottle of wine and poured two glasses. He looked up at me when he saw me walk in the room.

"You look lovely."

"Thank you. I figured I could slip into something a little sexy tonight while we enjoy our drink."

"I don't mind it at all," Anthony motioned for me to come sit on his lap, and I obeyed.

I gave him a long kiss on his lips, while I picked up my glass of wine and took a sip. I picked up Anthony's glass as well and allowed him to sip from his. After a long day of walking, playing and enjoying each other, this was the perfect way to spend the evening.

"So, what did she say about me earlier?" Anthony asked.

"What do you mean?"

"I know how girls are. Once you get a moment alone, the girl talk begins. And when we were getting ready for dinner, I heard you guys talking, but I couldn't tell what you guys were saying."

I laughed at him, "so, you were spying on us?"

"No, no, no.. not like that. Just saying, I could hear the muffled voices, and I can only assume that you were picking Chelsea's brain for information about if she liked me. So come on, tell me. I have to know!"

"Ok, ok! I will say, she loves you! She said you were very sweet and fun to be around. And the dessert definitely pushed you over the edge into the coolest person ever category."

Anthony smiled, "well that's great! I'm so glad she likes me. I've been nervous about it all day; wanting to make a good impression on her. I know she's a big part of your life, and her opinion matters."

"Well, you made the best impression babe. She loves you, and so do I."

Anthony leaned in, put my glass on the table and started kissing me. I returned all the loving he had to offer and more. Eventually, we decided to take our night cap into the bedroom, and cuddle while we finished watching tv and drinking our wine. The more Anthony kept making me feel like a queen, the more I knew that he was probably the one I could see myself with for a long time.

The next morning, Anthony woke me briefly to tell me that he was going for a run around the block. I told him ok, and rolled back over and went to sleep. I could not understand how he was even able to move, let alone run after the day we spent in DC. My body was on fire, and sore in every place I could imagine. After he left, I checked my phone to see the time; it was 7:45am. I checked my notifications and saw that Nia had texted me last night, asking about the day. I sent her a text telling her if she was awake to call me and I would fill her in. She called as soon as she received the text.

"Hey girl!"

"Hey Nia, how are you?"

"I'm good girl, just letting Mariya run me crazy. But spill all the details, girl! How was the day? Does Chelsea like him or is he about to spend his absolute last night in DC?" My mind began to trail off to our events of the day. Every time I thought about it, I started to grin like a teenage girl who had just lost her v-card to the most popular boy in school.

"Well, Chelsea loves him. She said he was the best. And Anthony was adorable the entire day. He treated her like she was his own child; like we were a little family. He was the perfect gentleman; it honestly couldn't have gone any better than it did!"

"That's awesome! Ugh, now you guys can get married and have little babies!"

"Wait Nia! I wouldn't put us down the aisle just yet."

"Shit, why not!? You might as well be thinking in that direction. I'm not saying you start demanding a ring from him tomorrow, but let's face it; you ain't gettin' any younger, girl. These are the prime years that we are vetting partners for the 'forever and always' type life. We too old to be playing house with people we have no future with."

"Very true, sis. Very true."

"I'm just saying; from what you've told me, it sounds like this is a man who you could see yourself being with for a long time. It seems to me like you may want to start looking at your options, because Anthony seems like the package deal."

"Yea, you're right. Anthony is sweeping me off my feet, which makes this hard because I don't want to rush it in any way. But I feel like I need to go ahead and strike while the iron is hot with this one. I don't want him to get tired of me."

"I agree with you, sis. Go on and get your man, girl. Y'all are beautiful together and you don't need to let that man get with anyone else."

"Well, I think I'm doing a good job of keeping him. So don't worry, I think I've got him under my spell."

We both laughed and then I ended the call with her. I text Anthony and asked him if he could bring me a coffee on his way back from his run, if he went in that direction. He text back and said he would.

Time always felt like it moved in slow motion when I was with Anthony. In just the short time that Anthony and I spent together, I feel like we have developed a routine that could last a lifetime. He was very in tune to my needs, Chelsea's needs, and seemed to fit perfectly in our lives. Nia loves him so far; and my mom seems to be interested in my business (or at least what I've told her so far), so I know eventually we would have to cross the next hurdle of our relationship; meeting family. More importantly, it was important for me that Trey knew that I had found someone else and am officially dating; and eventually, he will have to officially meet my mother.

It felt as though we were living in a fantasy movie. He'd come visit me, we'd spend time with Chelsea, he'd love me down every moment we got. When I'd visit him, he showed me around California, took me to sights I never thought I'd see; it was everything I needed and more. When we first got together, I thought it would just be a bi-coastal fling; something and someone to do whenever I was on the West Coast and needing a little something to get me by. But Anthony became far much more than that quicker than I thought he would be. We would sit up for hours and talk about our families, past experiences and anything else under the sun. For a long time after Trey, I never thought I would be able to love or be loved. This was more than a breath of fresh air. Anthony was beginning to become the air I needed.

I knew that it was time to start having "the talk" with Anthony. Specifically, the "we are official, and I'd like to be exclusive" talk, because if this is going to lead us into a future together, there are a few things we really need to discuss; like meeting Trey.

About an hour later, Anthony came knocking at my door from his run. I jogged to the door and opened it for him. Every time I saw him, I never got over how fine he was. He was standing at my door in his Nike Pro shirt, which fit tightly over his bulging shoulders and arms. He was wearing basketball shorts and running shoes. Sweat was dripping from face and his head was glistening. He was fine as hell.

He chuckled at me while I drooled over his body, "are you going to let me in or not?"

"Oh, yea. Sorry babe."

"I know you can't resist me, baby. I try to stay in shape for you."

"I appreciate it."

He walked in, kissed me on the forehead and headed to my kitchen to grab some water. He stood in my kitchen and took long gulps of water to hydrate himself. As he did this, I launched into my declaration about our exclusivity.

"So, I think I'm going to go ahead and tell my mom about us, since you've met Chelsea and everything. I think I'm ready for that next step."

He raised his eyebrows mid-gulp. As he finished his water and threw the bottle in the trash, he asked, "what took you so long?"

"What do you mean?"

"I already told my dad about you."

"Really?"

"Yea. He's like my best friend though. And when something big happens in my life, I need his input."

I walked over to him, "Oh; so I'm 'something big?'"

"Yes. I knew it the first time we went out. I told him that night. I told him that I was planning on being serious with you. And I needed his advice."

"Well what did he say?"

"That's a man's secret, babe. Can't give you my entire playbook," he said. He gave me another kiss and walked towards my bedroom to take a shower. On his way there, he yelled, "go ahead and tell your mom about me. I think it's time!"

I smiled, grabbed my phone and proceeded to dial her number. She answered after the second ring.

"Hey ma"

"Hey baby, how are you?"

"I'm good. What ya up to?"

"Oh nothing, just up watching these stories. What you doing, gal?"

"Just thinking about some stuff. I gotta tell you about Anthony."

"Who's Anthony?"

I looked at my phone like I saw my mama grow two heads through it, "mama! You know the guy I told you about that I had met in LA? The one I've been seeing?"

"Oh, yea...I remember him. I thought that was just something casual."

"Well.... I thought so too, but now, it seems like we may be moving towards being more exclusive. I let him meet Chelsea."

I heard a long pause, "really? He met Chelsea already?"

"Yea ma. He came to visit recently and met her. It went really well. She likes him a lot."

"Oh... well, that's good baby girl. I'm happy if you're happy," she said.

"Are you sure?"

"What you mean?"

"You don't sound happy, ma. You sound unsure."

"I just want to make sure you're sure about this, Chante. What does Trey think about all this? I mean, Chelsea is HIS daughter."

"Mama, I know you worship the ground Trey walks on, but Trey has moved on. And I haven't told him yet, but I plan on it. He hasn't considered how Chelsea feels about being married to the woman who Chelsea has called her auntie all her life."

My mother was silent. I mean, what the hell could she say? It was the truth.

"Look ma, I know I am the wrong one here, but when are you going to stop holding the torch for Trey? I know I was wrong; I know you're disappointed, but don't I deserve to find new love as well? Trey has not and is not coming back to me. This family is no more, and I did that, so we just have to move on, Ok?"

My mother sighed, "I know baby. I just love Trey. He was a good man; a great man honestly. They don't really make them like that anymore. Sometimes I do wish one day he would leave that ho Liyah and come back to you and Chelsea and y'all be a family again."

I felt a smile creep onto my face, "trust me ma, I do too sometimes. But that chapter is closed; and I have a right as a woman to find new love. I might have found it with Anthony. I think you will like him. He's a good man. I plan on bringing him home for Christmas."

"Oh. Well that would be nice...but, Trey is probably coming over too."

I paused, "that'll be fine. Trey will know about him by then. We're all grown; if I can be in the same room with Trey and Liyah, he can be in the same room with Anthony and I."

"Well alright then baby! I gotta go, my show is almost over and I'm going to have to rewind because you talked me to death," my mama said as she laughed.

I laughed in unison with her, "my bad mama. Go watch your shows. I'll talk to you later. Love you."

"Love you too. And Chante?"

"Yes mama?"

"I truly am happy for you."

She hung up the phone. I smiled and put my phone down. My mom is a stubborn one, and she doesn't like change. When Trey and I split up, she was very upset with me. She couldn't understand how I could mess up "the best thing that's ever happened to me." It helps to know that she's trying to turn her opinion around. Christmas will be the deciding factor; if Anthony can get through a holiday with the Thomas family, he's in there for life.

FOURTEEN

"Girl, I told mama about Anthony."

Nia and I were engaging in our new tradition, lighting up a fat blunt in the park, Nia taking photos and me editing submissions. Nia's sister had agreed to watch Mariya and Chelsea on Sundays while we fired up our creative juices and found our 'higher' purpose. Nia was deep into the zone while I was running my mouth about my conversation with my mom, trying to gauge her feelings about Anthony. I don't know if Nia was listening to me or not, but I could hear her shutter going a mile a minute.

"Did you hear me?"

"Yea girl; what did moms say, was she happy?"

"Honestly, she is still stuck on Trey. She is not down with change. Trey was like the son she never had, and when we divorced, it broke her heart. Trey has never treated her any different. In his eyes, that's still 'ma', but my mom still knows there's a disconnect there."

"She'll come around. Anthony is awesome. If the man is treating you right, your mom will come around. Moms never really care in the end as long as their baby is being treated right. So, by Christmas, that eggnog is hittin', all she is going to be worried about is that you're happy!"

I laughed, "you're right girl. I am not even going to trip about it."

I took the last drag on my blunt and put my red pen down. I needed a break and wanted the herbs to do their job while I soaked up some vitamin D. Nia had come over and handed me her camera; a new habit of hers. She always wanted my opinion on her shots when I was with her. I appreciated that she valued it, even though I didn't know a damn thing about photography.

"Tell me what you think," she said.

I sat up and looked at the shots. They were amazing. I always admired the way Nia was able to capture certain moments with the camera. She was great at her craft.

"They look great, Nia! What are you shooting for?"

"Really? Just because. I don't do enough shooting for fun. Just trying to find some fun in it all because sometimes I lose the joy in it, ya know?"

"I feel you. I feel that way about writing all the time. I get so caught up in the work that I lose the joy of creating. So I definitely feel you."

"Sooo, I have something to tell you," Nia said. She sat next to me.

"What happened?"

"Remember the little situationship I was telling you about a while back; with the girl I met in Atlanta?" she said, and covered her face with her hands like a school girl.

"Um, yea; I remember. What happened with that? You haven't mentioned her in a while," I said, laying back onto the blanket we laid out.

"Well, we had been keeping it super casual for a while, but I'll admit I have been lowkey sneaking her up here to spend time with her and going down there."

"Really now? So, you been sneaking around on me now, miss Nia?" I said with the side eye.

She laughed, "yea just a little bit. But honestly, Chante, I wanted to make sure it was right. And since I don't talk to my parents like that, you're the only person who's opinion I value about my relationship, and I wanted to make sure she was legit. So far, she's passed all the tests."

"Well in that case, when's the next time she's coming to visit?"

"She'll actually be here this weekend."

"Really?! In that case, y'all are having dinner at my house Saturday night. If she means this much to you, then I've got to meet her. And she's got to have my famous lasagna."

"You're right. I think it's time. I'm starting to fall pretty hard for her. She is amazing, Tae. I haven't felt this way about anyone in a long time. So I think I need her to pass the best friend test, and then she will be in there."

"I'm so excited! Saturday it is then! We're having our first little dinner party!"

Saturday had arrived, and there I was, cooking dinner with the music blasting. I was excited to be meeting Nia's new girlfriend. I could tell she was nervous, but I told her I would make it a great evening of good food and drinks and hopefully gaining a new friend. She was happy that she had finally found someone to make her happy. I decided that I would make what Nia called, my "world famous, deserved an award" lasagna. I didn't think it was all that great, but everyone including Nia absolutely loved it. Even Trey would want me to make it at least twice a month. As I was cooking, I had a bottle of wine open and one on chill for when Nia and her girlfriend arrived. The night was shaping up to be a great one, and I had to admit it felt pretty nice hosting a small get together; I hadn't done it in so long.

As my Ari Lennox playlist was transitioning from one song

to the next, the doorbell rang. I grabbed the remote and turned the music down.

"Coming!"

I walked over to the door to open it. Nia was there beaming with joy, "hey girl!"

"Hey sis! How are you?"

"Honestly, I'm nervous as hell. I feel like I'm 18 or something coming out to my parents," Nia said anxiously.

"Don't be silly, Nia. I'm sure she will be awesome, and I will love her. Where is she anyway?"

"Parking the car. Matter of fact, she's coming up the stairs now," she said.

I peeked through the doorway to see when she would come up. When I saw her, I'm sure my eyes got wider than I could ever imagine, because hers did too. I couldn't believe who I was staring in the face, I was completely speechless.

When she walked up the stairway to my door, Nia embraced her and put her hand gently around her waist, "Chante, this is my girlfriend, Tara."Stunned was the best way I could describe it. Tara Mitchell was back in my life, in my apartment, with my new best friend as her partner.

Tara shared my surprised expression; we tried to hide it, but I wasn't sure if we were that good at it. Nia caught on to us and said, "you guys alright?"

Tara snapped out of her trance, "yea. I'm good, sorry."

"So, we're not going to acknowledge that we know each other?" I thought.

"Good. I am going to run to the bathroom, Chante. Then if you want, we can get started on this dinner. It smells amazing."

"Right! Sure Nia, go ahead, I'll make sure Tara makes herself at home," I said with a glance at her. She looked back at me, not wavering in the discomfort sitting in her chest.

Nia walked up the hallway to the bathroom; and I was then left with Tara.

"So?" I said.

"So..." Tara said, with a smirk.

"Never thought I'd be seeing you again. How are you?" Tara said, going in my kitchen. It was like we never stopped being friends, she knew exactly where the wine was and grabbed a glass.

"I see you've not changed, T. You're all in my kitchen," I laughed.

"And you haven't changed because you always have a kitchen full of wine," she said. We both laughed; it felt like we hadn't lost a minute of time.

Tara laughed as well, "I guess old habits die hard. And I've been good, clearly."

"Clearly."

There was an awkward pause. It's almost like we were trying to find the words to make up for the moments lost. The words to make up for the wounds that were put in our lives so long ago. The one thing that cause us both so much pain.

I broke that shaky ice first, "Tara, I..."

"Tae', don't. I've moved on. I don't want to go back to that part of my life. I've forgiven you and him for that part of my life. You've moved on; I've clearly moved on. I just want to really stay happy. Nia makes me happy for right now. Honestly, I don't know where it will go from here, but right now, I am happy, and I want to stay happy for once."

"Well in that case, I will just give you a hug, and move on," I said, walking over to her. I opened my arms and embraced her. She returned the embrace. It felt good to have Tara back in my life. There was at least one person I can say I could mend the past with; maybe not Liyah, but at least Tara and I could maybe find our place again.

"So, how is Liyah?" she asked.

"Liyah and I don't speak," I said as I went to the oven to check my garlic bread.

"Really?!"

"She's with Trey. They have a son."

"Are you fuckin' kidding? She has a baby with him? Aw shit, I'm going to need some more wine for this."

"Who has a baby?" Nia said as she walked in the kitchen with us.

We both froze. I looked at Nia. We were caught red handed and we were going to have to admit at this point that something was up. Nia was looking at us like we were crazy, so I knew she was going to need an explanation. Tara spoke first.

"Babe, we kind of have a confession to make," she said as she walked over to her and wrapped her arm around my shoulder.

"Wait, y'all together or something? Chante, you taking my girl behind my back?"

"Girl hell no! I have a man and I'm very happy!" I said laughing, "but I am *very* familiar with your girlfriend."

Nia looked at me with a raised eyebrow.

"Chante and I knew each other in Atlanta, " Tara said, "we lost touch for a little while when she moved, but I guess now that I am relocating, we are going to link back up here pretty soon," she said smiling at me.

"Ohhhh, wow! This is the smallest world ever! My bestie and my baby girl are already cool? Well, this is my lucky day! Now I don't have to waste time trying to get y'all to like each other! That's one thing off my to-do list!" Nia said. We all laughed.

"Yea, we used to be thick as thieves; me, Chante and Liyah." Tara said.

"Who's Liyah?" Nia asked. Nia knew that Trey had married another woman, she had no idea it was my old best friend.

Tara giggled and took a big gulp of her wine. I looked over at Nia, "Just someone we know from back in Atlanta. An old friend who was waaay out in the streets. We never thought she would settle down and have kids, and boom! She had a baby!" I said.

"Oh, I see. Well, I'm hungry, and you both have already started drinking, and I'm trying to get there, so let's have some fun tonight!" Nia went into the kitchen to pour herself a glass of wine.

Tara and I looked at one another, she whispered, "is your number still the same?"

I nodded. Tara sent me a text at that moment, so I would have her new number.

"We will have to talk about all this later. Meet me tomorrow?"

I nodded again at her and smiled. I sent her a text of the Starbucks around the corner from my house. We would get coffee and talk.

Nia came from the kitchen and grabbed Tara by the waist. She placed a kiss on her cheek and took a sip of her wine. I was so happy for her and Tara, happier that Tara was able to find happiness and now knowing she forgave me was putting me more at ease. Tara was back, and a little piece of me was becoming whole again.

FIFTEEN

The next day, I texted Tara after we exchanged numbers to meet up with her. Seeing her really made me feel good, and since meeting at my house didn't cause World War III, I decided to extend an olive branch and see if she wanted to do lunch with me. When she texted me back and said she'd love to, I was elated.

We met a couple hours after that, at the Starbucks around the corner from my house. When we saw each other, we embraced the way we didn't have a chance to at my house.

"I'll just say it; I missed you Tara," I said squeezing her as I hugged her.

"I missed you too, Chante."

"I don't even know where to start! We have so much to catch up on. I hope you've got time."

"Oh, I've got tons of time. Let's grab this coffee and get to it," Tara said as she sat at the table.

Tara wasted no time filling me in on the details of her life. As far as she knew, Channing was in jail still, and after all of the legal proceedings, she decided to move and get a restart on life. Her and Josh pretty much cut off all communication with Channing, despite his attempts to write and contact them. He sent letters to their old address, that were forwarded to the new ones, and even wrote his family, who tried to call Tara to deliver messages. Tara had no idea what he wanted to say, because she never took the calls, and never opened the letters. Every time she got one, she threw it away. Tara knew the only way to truly get rid Channing and that chapter of her life, was to completely cut off all ties.

"I can't lie; for a long time, I missed him. I missed having a partner to share my life with. I hated that Josh didn't have his father in his life, but I knew that this was the only way to keep him and I safe. He has moved on, and now that he is a little older, I am able to give him a little more insight on what happened with Channing and I. He gets sad sometimes, but he gets over it eventually."

"Well, that's wonderful Tara. Sounds like you guys have been able to bounce back from all of that drama. Now, what I want to know is how you and Nia found one another."

Tara took a sip of her coffee and smiled. Just the sound of her name seemed to light Tara up in a way that I never saw with Channing. I enjoyed seeing that happiness.

"So, Nia was visiting Atlanta one weekend sometime last year. I went out to a club with my sister and I saw her there. Oddly, I couldn't keep my eyes off her. And she couldn't keep her eyes off me either. She walked over to me, asked me my name and we started talking. I didn't want to admit that I was attracted to her, obviously, but it was something about her that I was completely gravitated to. Before I knew it, I was all in. She had me from that first night."

"Wow. That's crazy! It's such a small world. I met Nia during a photoshoot up here in DC. As soon as I started talking to her, we clicked. We've been hanging out ever since."

"I don't know what it is, Chante. She brings me so much joy; joy that I didn't even feel when I was with Channing. At first, I thought I was having some delayed reaction to having a rebound person. But I just let it happen. I didn't try to stop fate. I let everything flow between me and her, and now we are as close to perfect as things can get. I even decided to relocate up here to be closer to her.

"Seriously?! You're going to be up here permanently?!" I asked.

"Yes. I figure this is the best option for me. Atlanta was starting to suffocate me. Between all that has happened there and Channing's family down my throat, it's better for me to move now. I need a fresh start and that begins with me letting go of Atlanta for the foreseeable future."

I couldn't lie, I was excited. To have Tara eventually living in the same area was nice to hear. My circle could be growing a little bit at a time, if she would consider us being closer again, in due time.

Tara took another sip of her coffee and asked, "So, I never got to tell you that I had to officially cut Liyah off after we all went through all of that drama."

"What happened?"

"Well, it started off that we were fine. We would talk a little here and there, but eventually, all she would talk about is you, what you were doing and if you were plotting to steal Trey back from her. She would always say, 'I don't know what she's capable of anymore, so I have to watch my man *and* my back.' Eventually I would tell her to not worry about you and live her life, because obviously you were living yours; but she wouldn't let go. It was crazy. I finally just had to start creating some space between us, until finally we stopped talking altogether. She would still try and blow up my phone, but I just ignored her until she stopped. I'm not sure who she found to annoy with that nonsense, but I'm glad it's not me anymore."

I just sat there in shock. I couldn't believe Liyah was running around throwing my name in the mud like she was completely innocent. I mean, I know I did some foul shit, but she is the one who has now got pregnant by my (then) husband, and then tried to claim it as revenge.

"I never knew if our paths would cross again, let alone like this; but I wanted to tell you that I forgive you, Chante. Channing was very manipulative and toxic and I'm just glad we all got away from him. He was bad for the both of us."

"You're right, Tara. What I did was unforgivable, and I am so grateful that we are able to move past it. I want you to know that I never meant to hurt you and what I did was completely unnecessary."

We hugged one another tightly, a hug that solidified peace being made in each of our lives. We finished our coffee and went our separate ways that day, but she promised she would let me know when she was officially moved in with Nia.

SIXTEEN

"Chelsea, have you packed your suitcase yet?"

"Ummmmm, almost!"

"That sounds like you haven't started yet, Chels. We're leaving in the morning, and you won't have any clothes to wear when you go visit your dad for Fall break." I yelled at her.

Chelsea was preparing to spend the week with her father for her fall break. She was also going to spend time with his parents. She was excited since she didn't get to see them very often. Trey typically would take her straight to Florida, so since she had a few extra days for this break, Trey agreed that he would stay in Atlanta and allow his parents to spend time with her as well. Chelsea couldn't stop talking about all the things she and her "GiGi" were going to get to do when she got to Georgia. I couldn't get her to hush up about it!

I walked towards her room to make sure she was putting the clothes in her bag that I picked out for her and when I walked in, she was fast asleep on top of her bed. It looked as if she fell asleep in mid-pack. I laughed to myself, "she must have tired herself out with all that excitement."

I proceeded to pack up the remainder of her stuff and place her bags by the door. I set my alarm and decided to call it night, but not before I sent Anthony my usual goodnight text. He replied back and asked if Chelsea was all ready for her trip.

"Yep," I replied back, "she fell asleep on me, so I finished packing up for her. So, we'll be hitting the road bright and early."

"Good. Get some rest, babe. I'll call you in the morning on your way out."

"But it's going to be 6am, love. That's three a.m. your time."

"I know. I have an alarm set to make sure you're on the road."

I rolled my eyes while blushing, *"why does he treat me like this?"* I sent him a kissy-face emoji and put my phone on the charger. I had an early morning, and I had to get some shut eye.

The next morning, like clockwork, Anthony called and wished us safe travels as we got ready to head to Atlanta. Chelsea and I loaded up the car, put on our favorite tunes and hit the highway. While we were on the way there, I decided to ask Chelsea about how she felt about Anthony, after meeting him for the first time a few months ago.

"He's ok. But he's not daddy. Is he going to be my new daddy, mommy?" Chelsea asked. I was taken aback by her question, but I truthfully couldn't put it past her, she was smarter than your average five-year-old.

"No sweetie, no one could ever replace daddy. He will always be your daddy. Mr. Anthony is just a friend that mommy enjoys spending a lot of time with right now. He makes her happy."

"But mommy, why can't daddy make you happy? Is it because he is with Auntie Liyah?"

"I knew this day would come eventually," I thought. I swallowed hard and prepared to try and answer this question without further traumatizing my already traumatized daughter.

"It's a little complicated, sweetie. Yes, daddy is currently with Auntie Liyah, so he is not allowed to make mommy happy. When mommy and daddy were together, mommy tried to let someone else make her happy, and it made daddy very upset with me; and that is why we are not together now. Daddy has found someone to make him happy, and I have found someone new to make me happy."

"Oh." Chelsea said, with a sound of disappointment in her voice. I knew Trey and I not being together had negatively affected Chelsea; and with the way things have panned out, I can see why she doesn't understand it. One minute, she has a loving auntie and a happy mom and dad; then, her auntie is now her 'other mommy' as she calls her, and mommy and daddy are not happy with each other.

"Chelsea, I want you to know that mommy and daddy will always love you, no matter what. It's just that the idea of mommy and daddy being together just didn't work anymore. We still care about each other and are friends, but we just are not in a relationship like we were."

"I get it mommy. I guess one day this will all make sense, because it's confusing!" she exclaimed.

I let out a hearty laugh. My daughter's personality was a force to be reckoned with. You never know what she is going to say. I couldn't believe just how in tune she was to life at such a young age. I looked up into my rearview mirror and saw that she had gone back to watching her movie on Netflix, with her headphones on, which meant to me that she was done with whatever conversation we were having.

"Thank God," I thought. That conversation was getting heavier than I was comfortable with. While she watched her movie, I put my music up and continued to fly down the highway to Atlanta.

After a long eight-hour drive, I finally pulled up to Trey's mother's home. I couldn't have been happier to stop driving for the day. As soon as I turned the car off, I could see Ms. Wright's door opening and her coming out to greet us.

"Hello to my beautiful girls!" Ms. Wright said as she came over to the car. It really made me feel special that she still considered me one of her girls, even though Trey and I aren't together.

"Hey Mama Wright. How are you doing? You're lookin' good!" I said. Chelsea jumped out of the car and ran up to her grandmother and gave her a big hug. Mama Wright picked Chelsea up and gave her a million kisses.

"Oh, I'm fine, dear. Just glad to see you all made it safely, and my partner in crime is here now," she said smiling.

"Granny, can I go finish watching my movie?" Chelsea said.

"Sure baby. Go ahead to your room."

When Chelsea ran into the house, I stood there with Trey's mother, and even after so many times of seeing her since the divorce, each time continued to feel awkward. I knew she felt how awkward I was with her, but she didn't care.

"Come here, Chante. Give me a hug, baby."

I walked over and gave her a long, tight squeeze. Before I let go, she said to me, "I don't know why you act like you're a stranger."

"Well Mama Wright, technically, I am a stranger now. I am not your daughter-in-law anymore."

"Oh please! I don't care what's happened between you and Trey, you are my first and ONLY daughter-in-law. That other girl, she's just something Trey decided to play with when his feelings got hurt. And I'm not saying that he shouldn't have been hurt, because you needed your ass whooped too; but really? Your best friend Chante? He knew that shit was messed up, excuse me." she said.

"Wow," I thought. I had to laugh to myself; Mama Wright

was really letting it all out.

"I appreciate that, Mama. And trust me, I know I am beyond wrong, I just wish it was anyone else but her. I could have gotten over it by now, but it continues to hurt more than I'd like it to."

I lowered my head, ashamed of my past once again. Trey's mother pulled my head up and told me, "don't you hang your head. If anything, she should be ashamed for betraying your friendship like that. I told Trey she wasn't nothin' but a home-wreckin' ho. Liyah could've kept that between y'all and instead she stuck her nose in y'all business and now look; she done went and had a damn baby with Trey and all! Lord, let me hush. I love TJ with all my heart, but the way he got here wasn't right, and I'm not ashamed to say it, but I won't ever say it in front of him," she said laughing. I laughed right along with her. I let her vent about the situation in whatever way she chose. I wasn't one to judge her one bit.

Just as we were enjoying our inside joke, Trey pulled up next to my car. He got out, and I couldn't lie, he was looking good. We locked eyes as he was walking up to me, and I quickly looked away. I didn't want him to get any ideas. It pained me that the chemistry still seemed to simmer slowly between us sometimes.

Trey's mother must have caught it, because after she kissed her son on the cheek, she said that she was going inside to check on Chelsea. Now, it was just Trey and I, in each other's space.

"Well, hey there!" I said casually. I tried to keep things light.

"Hey Chante, how are you?"

"I'm doing ok. How about you? How's the baby and Liyah? Are they coming?"

"Nah. Liyah is still in Miami with TJ. He is starting a new daycare this week, so of course one of us had to stay. They are doing pretty good though, nothing too out of the ordinary I guess."

"Oh ok. Got it."

Another long, awkward silence.

"So, I see you glowing, Chante. How's life been treating you?" He was eyeing my frame, only assumingly impressed.

I laughed lightly as I answered him, "Life is going very well for me actually. Nothing to complain about really. So, I guess that glow you see could just be me living my best life," I said. I wasn't quite ready to let Trey know that I had been involved with someone, but I made the decision that prior to us traveling home for Christmas, I would let Trey know that I had someone since I would be bringing him home to meet my mother. I at least did not want to spring a new man on him, so giving him a heads up should be ok.

"That's good, that's good. I'm glad to hear it."

I looked at Trey and could tell there was something he wanted to say but wasn't saying it. His body language shifted a bit and he was trying hard not to make eye contact with me.

"Well Trey, I guess I will let y'all go get your week started. Have fun and don't spoil our baby too much." I began to walk to my side of the car, when Trey grabbed my arm.

"Wait, Chante. Can I say something?"

"Um, yea. What's on your mind?"

"I don't really know how to say this, so I'm just going to say it. There are days when I'm at home, and I think about you. I think about us and what we had, and I miss it. I can't lie about it, I miss the good times we had, and seeing you this happy without me, without our life, it's weird to me."

"Uh, wow Trey; I don't really know what to say about that.

I mean, I would be lying if I said I didn't miss the times we had as well. But I still can't get past the hurt. I mean, of all people, Trey, you picked the one person you knew that would hurt me; you married her, and had a baby with her. I can't look past that. I know I was wrong, but I honestly could have been ok with it being any other woman on this planet but Liyah."

Trey mumbled something under his breath, and I asked him to repeat it, "what did you say?"

"I said I wish I would have thought that through when I made that choice," He said, finally finding the courage to look me in the eye.

I could feel something in me wanting to reach out to him. Hearing him say those words literally took my breath away. As much as I wanted to fall into his arms again, something stopped me. The fact that I was falling for Anthony allowed pause, *"I can't repeat this cycle. I'm with Anthony now, and I'm happy. I have to let Trey go,"* I thought to myself.

"That's really flattering, Trey, but you know we really can't turn back time now. You're married to Liyah now; and I am finally happy. We are both in a comfortable place in life right now and we cannot change that."

"So, is someone making you happy these days, or is that really just 'life' giving you that glow for real?"

"Definitely just living my best life right now, Trey. But if that changes, I'll decide if I'll be ready to let you know. Out of respect, I would want to let you know if I am dating and if they've met Chelsea. But for right now, just know I've been happy lately."

I stood firm in my decision that I would not allow the words Trey was telling me to sway me from my feelings. I had Anthony and I was back in a very good place. I wasn't going to let Trey's mixed emotions screw up everything I have built back up for my life.

Trey looked at me like a sad puppy. He was defeated, and he knew it. "You're right, Chante. We can't go back now. And I won't try to press for information. You can't help a brother for trying to see; because you're definitely looking good these days. But I just wanted you to know that I will never forget some of the best years of my life, and I have learned from them. I know I had my faults too and I see that now. I want you to know that I am changing into a better man."

"I'm glad to hear that," was all I said.

I went inside to tell Chelsea I was finally leaving the house and to be good with her father. When I got outside, we exchanged good-byes at that moment and then I got into my car. As I was pulling out of Trey's mother's driveway, I could see Trey continuing to stare at me; wishing he had that old thing back. As much as I wished it too sometimes; my heart has moved on.

On my way home, I moved on to more important matters, like planning Anthony and I's first Christmas together; which was going to be important, because he'd be meeting my mother. This was a pretty big deal for me, because I had only merely spoke about Anthony casually, and my mother didn't really know just how serious we had gotten so fast; however, I want her to know. Anthony was on the phone with me as I drove back to DC. I didn't tell him about the awkward conversation with Trey. I decided to leave that right in his mother's driveway along with a lot of other feelings. I talked to Anthony all the way home.

"So, I need to let you know that Trey will probably be at my mother's house for Christmas. Our families are still so close that they still come by to eat, so he and Liyah may be there with their son."

"Oh, ok. Cool," he said.

I waited for more commentary but got nothing, "that's it?

That's all you have to say?"

"Yea. That doesn't bother me, babe. I'm with you and I have a purpose to be there, meet your mother and spend Christmas with my woman. Trey doesn't intimidate me."

"Well, I didn't think he did intimidate you, I just wanted you to know that he was going to be there. I would hate to have both of you in the same place and not say anything and it be really awkward."

"I appreciate you letting me know Chante, but trust me, he's not on my radar. The only person on my radar is you."

That put a smile back on my face.

"I also want to tell you that I am going to let Trey know that you will be with me. He doesn't know that I have been seeing someone, so this will be the first time he is finding out about you."

"Again, that's cool babe. Whatever you need to do. It's very respectful of you so I'm not going to stop you."

Once I got off the phone with Anthony, I sent Trey a quick text.

"Hey, I have a confession, I have been seeing someone for a while now and I will be bringing him to meet mom. I wanted you to know."

I waited for a response; unsure of what type or if I will even get a response at all. In about five minutes, my phone buzzed.

"Oh. Ok. I kinda knew that glow came from somewhere huh?" he wrote back.

"Yea, I guess so. I'm very happy. And he's meeting my mom so, it's getting pretty serious I guess."

"Has he met Chelsea?"

"Yes. She has, just recently."

"Oh. Aight."

That's the last text I got from him that night. I know Trey, so I know he was wounded. *"I don't know how he thought this was going to go,"* I thought.

SEVENTEEN

Anthony was adjusting his shirt collar in the mirror, almost as if he was preparing to take me out to the prom for the first time.

"Are you sure everyone is going to like me? I would never admit this to my boys, but I'm a little nervous," Anthony confessed to me as we pulled into my mother's driveway.

"Don't worry about it, babe. My mother will love you; and my family is not nearly as bad as I tend to talk about," I laughed. I admit I make my family sound like a bunch of brazen lunatics, who can be a little overwhelming to new people; but truthfully, they are harmless, and only want to see me happy.

My mother has been anticipating this meeting since I told her about Anthony two months ago. She was apprehensive at first, but I could tell she was willing to give it a try and that's all I could ask for at this point.

Anthony turned the keys off in the ignition and looked over at me, "You sure your family isn't going to run me off or anything like that?" he said.

I leaned over and kissed him softly on the lips, and then on the nose, "I promise, Ant. They are practically harmless. Let's go inside before my mom sees us and wonders why we aren't getting out of the car."

As we were walking up to the front door, I could see my mother opening the door, and her smile beamed from ear to ear.

"Hey baby! Merry Christmas!" she said excitingly.

"Merry Christmas mama!" I said to her, reaching out to

give her a hug. Anthony looked on, holding Chelsea's hand as I embraced my mother.

"Mama, this is Anthony, my boyfriend." Even as old as I was, it felt completely awkward introducing a boyfriend to my mother, especially since I had already been married.

"Well, hello there, Anthony. It is a pleasure to finally meet you," She said, giving him a once over. She looked him up and down, then looked at me and winked. "I've heard so much about you," she said to him. She could be pretty embarrassing sometimes.

"Hello Ms. Davis. Pleasure is all mine." Anthony said as he leaned in and kissed my mom on the cheek. I then noticed he leaned in and whispered to her, "I see Chante got all of her good looks from you."

My mother blushed so hard a blind man could see it. "Well, I haven't had a handsome man talk to me like that in a loooonnng time! I like him already, Chante. I might steal him from you!" she laughed.

I exchanged laughter with her, "Uh, yea, ok mom. Anyways, let's get in this house."

My mom walked in and we followed behind her. Anthony grabbed my hand as he led me into my mother's house. I whispered to him, "very smooth, Mr. Bishop."

He leaned back to me smiling, "you think so?"

"I would have to say so," I said in between giggles. I felt pretty good about the rest of my family meeting Anthony. If I could get him past my mom, the rest would be a piece of cake.

As the night went on, Anthony was a hit with my family! I was sneakily watching him from a distance as he got acclimated with my uncles, aunts and cousins. Everyone seemed to be having a great time with him and vice versa. I was sipping wine and talking to my mother as I watched him, with the biggest smile on my face. My mother noticed.

"You really like him, don't you Chante?"

"I do, mama. He's been nothing short of amazing since we started dating. It's like he doesn't penalize me for my past. He says that it's a new start for me and him, and we are leaving all that where it belongs; in the past."

"Well that is the best thing, baby. If he is willing to forgive the person you were, then he is a good man. How does Chelsea like him?"

"So far, they have gotten along great! He loves her like she is his own."

"Does Trey know that Anthony is here today?" my mother asked.

"I sent him a text and let him know; right after I let Anthony know that Trey was going to be here with Liyah. I didn't want any surprises, but just knowing Trey, I know he is bent out of shape about it."

Just as I was finishing up my glass of wine, I heard the doorbell ring. My mother hurried over to the door and opened it. That is when I saw Trey, Liyah and TJ at the door.

I poured another glass of wine and made sure it hit the very top of the glass.

"Here goes nothing." I said, preparing for a whole bunch of drama and bullshit once I saw the smirk

on Liyah's face.

Chelsea heard the door open, and when she saw it was Trey, her face lit up and she sprinted across the living room.

"Merry Christmas, daddy!" she said with a wide smile.

"Merry Christmas to you too, sweetie," Trey said.

"Merry Christmas, Chelsea!" Liyah said.

Chelsea looked over at Liyah, then to me. I gave her a wink, telling her it was ok to talk to her. Chelsea still didn't know how to process Liyah being with Trey when I was around.

"Merry Christmas Auntie Liyah," she said. I could tell that made Liyah upset. Chelsea would not call her "mom" for any reason under the sun. But how can you blame her, when her entire life, Liyah's been her aunt. I personally found it a little funny.

Trey leaned in and gave my mom a kiss on the cheek and a big hug, "Merry Christmas, ma." he said. I noticed he still was in the habit of calling her "ma." I never really bothered with it. As long as he has been calling her that, I imagine old habits die hard.

Trey scanned the room, looking for me. When we made eye contact, I gave him a faint smile. He just looked at me and looked away. *"still pissed I see."* I thought. Just then, Anthony came from the kitchen into the living room, placing his arm gently around my waist. When Trey saw that, he scoffed a little. He finally found his maturity and walked over to tell us hello.

"Hey Chante. Merry Christmas!" he said.

"Merry Christmas to you too Trey. How are you?" I asked. I could immediately feel the awkwardness between the three of us.

After Chelsea hugged her father, she went to play with TJ and the rest of her cousins.

What few seconds passed between us felt like hours in time. Anthony finally decided to be the first one to break the tense setting between the three of us.

"I'm Anthony. I assume that you are Trey; it's nice to meet you man. By the way, Chelsea is pretty much your twin," He said, as he extended his hand to shake Trey's.

"Hey man, you're right. I'm Trey. Merry Christmas," Trey said, with a slight apprehension in his tone.

They exchanged handshakes as I continued to drink in gulps.

"I'm not sure how much Chante has told you, but I'm her boyfriend," Anthony said.

"Yea.... she told me. Y'all look happy or whatever," Trey said, rolling his eyes slightly.

"So how long have you guys been seeing each other?"

"About seven months now," I said. I knew that would possibly throw him for a loop, since I am just now letting him know about Anthony.

"Oh really? Well, congrats you guys. I'm happy for the both of you," Trey said as he extended his hand to Anthony.

Anthony obliged and shook Trey's hand, "thanks man. That means a lot coming from you."

"Yea. I see you and Chelsea have a pretty good bond. Do you see her often?" Trey asked. I immediately felt a nervous sweat crawl down my back.

It seemed as if Anthony knew this was coming and played it very cool, "I just recently met her, so it hasn't been a lot of interaction, but I try not to overstep. I let Chelsea lead most of our interaction. I don't force myself into her life or try to take over a spot that's already been filled."

Another awkward pause between the three of us.

Trey finally looked over at me and said, "Mind if I talk to you for a minute?"

"Sure." I said. I poured another half glass of wine down and told Anthony I would be right back and proceeded to walk to the guest bedroom with Trey. Before I walked away, Anthony grabbed my wrist slightly, and took my wine glass.

"You don't need that. You're a grown woman. Handle your business."

I nodded at him and followed Trey.

As we walked towards my bedroom, my mother made eye contact with me. I assured her by mouthing *it's fine* so she wouldn't think anything. Truthfully, I knew Trey was taken aback and possibly pissed at being thrown off by what he didn't know about Anthony and me.

EIGHTEEN

When we got there, Trey wasted no time giving me a third degree. Clearly, he was not pleased.

"Really Chante?! Almost a year?! Y'all been dating for almost a year and you just now told me?"

"First of all, how is the length of time I date someone any of your business? How long were you fucking Liyah before I found out?"

"Don't pull that bullshit, Chante. This isn't about Liyah and I. This is about the fact that you let seven months pass by without telling me this man has been playing stepdaddy with my daughter!"

"Were you not listening? He *just* met Chelsea. Trey, I know you don't think much of me, but I didn't allow Chelsea to meet Anthony until after her birthday. She really hasn't known him that long and I would never keep this from you that long if Chelsea was that involved."

"Man, ok. Fine. Are you serious about this guy, Chante? This isn't just a fling that you have now exposed Chelsea to, and then you're gonna drop him in another month."

"You are asking a lot of questions for someone who doesn't have the privilege of knowing what the hell is going on in my life."

"Fine Chante. Just make sure you're serious about this, ok? There's no need in dragging Chelsea into something that won't last."

"Right Trey. Because you have made her life complicated

enough; what, with marrying her aunt and all."

Trey glared at me furiously. He knew this was a mess he created and now he couldn't undo. He took a sip of his drink and walked away. I took a deep breath, *"finally, that shit is over."* I sat down on the bed and began to process what exactly just happened. I couldn't believe that he spazzed out of me that bad, and even trying to place blame on me like I still belonged to him. I know we share a child together, but I never thought that he would care that much about who I was with.

Based on how he was acting, you would think Trey Wright still had feelings for me; because he was acting like a damn fool.

I walked back out to the living room with Anthony, who was playing with the kids on the living room floor. He looked up at me, almost as if to ask if everything was ok. I nodded at him and smiled. I picked my drink up off the table and took a sip.

Anthony walked over to me and gave me a kiss on the cheek.

"I'm fine baby. Let's enjoy the rest of our day."

The rest of the day went on pretty smoothly. Trey and Liyah only spent a few more hours at my mother's home, and when it was time to eat, they decided to go to his mother's house for the rest of the day. I agreed to let Chelsea go with him, since she had already opened all of her gifts at my mother's house.

Anthony had gotten me a beautiful scarf and bracelet that he found in California. I remembered it because it was one I had seen in a store on one of my many visits. I didn't even think he remembered. I bought him a watch with an inscription, "love, C."

"Thank you, sweetheart, I do love you endlessly."

"You're welcome, Anthony. I knew you'd like it," I said.

"I actually love it. It's perfect, just like you."

I blushed. He was so corny sometimes. In the spirit of the season, I loved it.

Towards the end of the night, when all my cousins and Anthony were passed out all over my mom's home, I helped her clean up in the kitchen and made myself and Anthony a to-go plate. As I was drying the dishes she was washing, I decided to pick her brain about Anthony, since this was her first time meeting him.

"So mama, what do you think about him?"

"Well, I like him. He's very respectable; handsome, he appears to treat you right and you seem very happy."

I felt there was a but coming, so I inquired, "but....?"

"What do you mean?"

"I feel like there is a negative comment coming after that statement."

"No, no negative. I just want to make sure you and Chelsea are happy and ok with accepting him. You know she only has one daddy."

"Yes mama. We're big kids now. One of the first things Anthony knew about was Chelsea and Trey and he knew that I had a life before he even came into the picture. He is not trying to take Trey's place, but he is not going to run away from being a father figure in Chelsea's life either. Chelsea loves him and Anthony treats her very well. I haven't seen any issues. So far, everything has been just short of perfect."

"In that case, baby, if you're happy, then I'm happy."

We didn't really go further into it after that, but something told me that she didn't feel as happy for me as I would have liked her to. Either way, I figured she'll come around eventually. She didn't originally like Trey when I first brought him to meet her, and now she thinks he walks on water.

I took another hour and helped my mother clean up most of her home until she practically kicked me out.

"It's getting late, Chante. Y'all need to get back to the hotel so you can get some rest before you leave."

"You sure mama? You know we can just stay the night here; or I can let Chelsea stay with you."

"Sure baby, that'd be nice. I'll wake up in the morning and make some breakfast. Let Chelsea stay since she's already asleep in her room."

I gave my mother a kiss on the cheek, "thanks mama. And I know he's not Trey, and it will take some getting used to, but he is a sweetheart. You will love him."

"I'm sure I will. I guess it's still a little weird for me to see you both not joined at the hip. You know Trey is my baby. It took a while, but he is still my son."

"I will never take that away from you; but he moved on, and I need to as well. Just give Anthony a chance."

"I will, baby. I will."

I gave my mother another kiss on the cheek and a big hug. She hugged me back tight. I knew she was nervous for me; but just wanted to see me happy. She will see in due time that Anthony makes me happier than I've been in a long time.

I walked over to the couch and nudged Anthony's shoulder. He was knocked out after eating, laughing and watching football with my uncles and cousins. I nudged him again and he finally opened his eyes.

"Wake up, sleepy head. It's time to go."

"Ok..." he grumbled, "do you need help with Chelsea?"

"No. She's going to stay with my mom tonight. We can come get her tomorrow and get some breakfast. Mama is cooking again."

"Really? In that case, I'll be up early. Your mother can burn!"

We both laughed as we gathered our things, told my mother goodbye and got in the car to head out.

On the drive back to our hotel, I looked over at Anthony, "so.... what did you think?"

"Overall, your family is amazing. Your uncles are hilarious and so are your cousins. Trey on the other hand...." He said and laughed.

"What?"

"He is interesting. Him and Liyah. I don't know why they put so much energy into knowing your business."

"I'm not sure either, but I can assure you, I don't care even a fraction as much as they care about me. My only focus is my job, my man, my family and my small circle of support. Liyah and Trey Wright do not fall anywhere on that list anymore."

"Well, it's good that you're not letting them get to you. I can tell that Liyah tries hard to make you jealous or something, but you don't even pay her any attention. I find that quite entertaining."

"Yea well, I don't care for it. I wish she'd just get a life and leave mine alone."

"Anyway, you know what else had my utmost attention today?" Anthony said, grabbing my hand as it rest on the gear shift.

"What?"

"You. You looked amazing today. I couldn't keep my eyes off you, or my mind out of the gutter."

"You always know just what to say, huh? Is that all you ever think about Mr. Bishop?"

"When you look that good, I'm surprised you think I could think about anything else right now."

Anthony allowed his hand to roam from my hand to my thigh, and soon he was rubbing in between the two. As we were pulling into the parking lot of the hotel, I couldn't get the car in park fast enough. We rushed out of the car like two teenagers who had just snuck off from their parents' house. We were going to end our first Christmas together on a high note tonight.

NINETEEN

"So, I think it's time."

I was reading, *Baracoon* at the time, "time? Time for what?"

"Time for you to meet my parents."

I sat up in my bed and closed my book with a raised eyebrow, "your parents? Really? You ready for that?"

He chuckled, "isn't that what couples do, Chante? They meet each other's parents? I mean, I met your mom; it's only fair that I let you meet mine."

"Sorry; that came out really weird. Of course, I want to meet your parents! I didn't mean to imply that I wouldn't want to meet them."

"I know. But, meeting your family, made me realize that I think it's time that you meet my dad and stepmom. Plus, my dad has been hounding me about when he's going to be able to meet you since I told him about you."

"Oh, so you've been talking to your dad about me?"

"Don't get the big head, girl. I talk to my dad about everything; remember? He's like my therapist; my priest. He's pretty much my everything, man. He gets me through a lot. He's a great guy." I watched how he talked about his father. It was the sweetest thing. I could tell that his relationship with his father was something that he cherished.

"So, what about your mom? Do you talk to her about me?"

Silence. There was an awkward and very uncomfortable pause in the conversation. I hit a nerve.

"No. I don't talk to her about anything."

"Why not?"

"I just don't."

"Oh. Ok." I left it alone. Clearly that was a subject that he was not willing to discuss with me.

"My mom and I; we don't have a great relationship. She and my father have not been together for some time now. I was abandoned as a child; when I was four years old my mother took me to the police station, and she left me there. She left me there and told me that she was not coming to pick me up. She had gotten into an argument with my father because she and him had broken up and he was with another woman at the time; nothing serious but casually dating, but still taking care of me. She wanted them to be together, but my father said he didn't want to be with her. She went ballistic. I was young, but I remember a conversation she was having before we left the house. She was frantically screaming, talking about how she couldn't believe he wasn't there with her, and how he could treat her like this; and that she would 'show him'. So, to play games, she abandoned me. She pawned me off and played with me like a toy. My father thought it was a game until the police called him and told him I was at the police station. He immediately came and picked me up, got emergency custody and kept me ever since then. I never forgave my mother for that. I couldn't believe she would play with my emotions and with *me* like that; just to play games. I have never appreciated a woman who would use a child to play a game with a man before. So, our relationship has been very estranged."

I'm sure my mouth was hanging wide open as he spoke, "wow. Baby, I can't believe she would do something like that. How did you deal with that?"

"My dad put me in therapy. When I was old enough, he made sure I had an outlet to be able to process what I went through with my mother. I also learned later on that my mother was manic depressive. She was having a major episode, and that my father was a trigger for her. She had stopped her medication, started stalking him, she did a lot to try and get him to come back. My father also admitted that he had done a lot to try and make sure she stayed on top of her mental health and didn't allow her to be independent. He admitted later if he didn't create a crutch for her, she might have been able to manage it her for herself. When he left, she didn't have support and he blamed himself for a long time. We both needed some healing from the whole thing."

I grabbed his hand, "I'm glad you were able to get through it, baby. If you ever need anything, you know I'm here."

"Thanks, babe. I appreciate that, but I'm good. I've been good for a long time now. Every now and then I still see a therapist if I need to process some things. I honestly am not sure where my mother is these days, but I am ok with our relationship. I've made my peace with who she is and what we've been through. I hope she's well, and my life is amazing. I want to keep it that way. So I leave well enough alone. My father is remarried now, and my stepmother is a saint. She's an amazing woman. You'll meet her, too."

"Well it sounds like you've got it all under control. I guess we all have things in our lives that make us unique and strong. I admire the strength you have to persevere through that; you and your father both."

He leaned in and gave me a kiss on the cheek, "thank you babe. The things I've endured make me the man I am today."

"And I love every part of you."

"I love you too."

Anthony turned over and turned off the lamp on the

nightstand. He turned and faced the inside of the bed and looked at me, smiling. I decided that for the night, I was done reading. I burrowed down under my comforter and leaned into his chest. He kissed me on the forehead.

The next morning, I couldn't stop thinking about the possibility of meeting Anthony's parents. What he told me about the story about his childhood piqued my interest even more about learning more about his childhood. Part of me didn't want to pry, but I did want to know how much he was willing to tell me, and if this relationship was going to get serious, I felt like we needed to at least start having more serious conversations about deeper parts of ourselves.

By now we had moved to my living room couch, watching CNN, when I asked him, "so, when do you want us to make this trip to see your parents?"

"I'm not too sure yet. Since they live in Chicago, I'd have to find some time off work and make sure our schedules match up. I wouldn't want to take you away from work too long. I know how you get when you're away from your office. You start itching." He looked at me with a hint of sarcasm laced across his lips.

I rolled my eyes, "I just like to make sure my office is running like a well-oiled machine. I can't help it if I like to have my finger on the pulse of how my baby is running. I put a lot of my blood, sweat and tears into it. If I take my eyes off them, they may run it into the ground.

Anthony took a bite of his cereal, "don't you think if you had to watch them that hard, you shouldn't have hired them in the first place? I mean, not to make you doubt your staff or anything; but if it was me, I would want to be able to take a week off from my company, and be able to check in, but not be intertwined in every single move they make. That's why they have executive assistant's babe. They are made to make sure they keep your business running; and your assistant is amazing. I think she can keep your office running for a week if I pulled you away."

I thought about it and Anthony was right. I do tend to hover a bit. I couldn't help that I love my work so much. I get tied up in so many projects, that I don't really take the time to step away enough. Part of that is due to the divorce. I had to bury my idle time into something other than men. So, I buried it in work and writing. And now Anthony is trying to cure me. *"Maybe this trip to see Anthony's parents will be my own little test of letting go a bit,"* I thought to myself.

"I'll give it a shot. You're right, Adrienne is the best assistant I've ever had, and she manages the office better than anyone I've ever seen. Both of my assistants do. I think I can loosen the reigns a bit and see what a little leadership in their hands looks like."

"That's my girl," Anthony said. He took my bowl and got up to take it to the kitchen, gave me a kiss and I laid back on the couch. I looked at my phone and pulled up my email account. I was looking through and checking in on things; the exact thing that Anthony said I do too much of. As soon as I noticed it, I put my phone down.

"He's right. I am a work-a-holic," I thought. I pulled my magazine back off the coffee table and started reading again as Anthony came back into the living room.

"How's your magazine?"

"Pretty good. Nia has another spread in this issue. She's doing such great work. I'm glad to say I know her," I said with a cheesy grin on my face.

I gave him a kiss as he sat next to me and continued watching the news. Eventually he fell asleep on the couch as I laid underneath him. I had gotten too engulfed in my thoughts to fall asleep. My mind was still buzzing at the thought of meeting Anthony's parents. It was something I'd be mentally preparing for in the coming days, whenever he tells me when we go.

The next day while I was at work, Tara came to visit me while she was on her lunch break. I decided to let her drag me away from my desk for an hour and a half to catch up, and I wanted to give her the latest news I had about Anthony and him wanting me to meet his parents.

We were sitting at a restaurant a few blocks away from my office and I was telling her all the details.

"It sounds like you guys are doing great, Chante. You know this means he's going to ask you to marry him soon, right?" she said.

"I don't know, Tara. He has not dropped any hints; like, none! I don't know where his head is at right now."

"Trust me. Tae. If he's going to let you meet his parents, he's getting there. It's only a matter of time now," she said. Tara had this huge grin on her face. She was such a cornball. I took her word for it for now, but I was still just enjoying where I was with Anthony. I didn't know if I wanted to think about spending the rest of my life with Anthony if he hadn't even brought up the thought of it yet.

Talking to Tara made me continue to think about how happy I was with Anthony but wonder if I really deserved it. There were so many times I thought whether or not I really deserved to have a second chance to love again; and I keep thinking that Anthony is just *too* perfect. He has taken a real chance at love with me and I can't help but be appreciative because he has been everything I've needed and so much more. He's also been perfect with Chelsea and being so kind to her. As much as talk myself out of how good things are with Anthony, I know he's right for me. I know I should just take what the universe has given me, but it also makes me wonder if I should even deserve it in the first place.

That night when I got home, Anthony had told me that he

talked to his dad and had made arrangements for us to see him in about a week, if that was ok.

"Sure. I think I'm free next weekend. I am going to talk to Nia and see if she and Tara can watch Chelsea that weekend. I'm sure Josh and Mariya would love to hang out with her for the weekend."

"Perfect. I've got a good feeling about this, babe. My dad is really excited. He doesn't get very many opportunities to tell embarrassing stories about me, so this should be interesting."

"In that case, I can't wait."

About a week later, Anthony and I were in Chicago, minutes away from meeting his stepmother and father. As we were driving through the neighborhoods, my palms were getting sweaty and I could feel my heart beating out of my chest. I was so nervous. I really wanted his parents to like me, because they meant a lot to him. And with my mom showing some apprehension, I needed his parents to be supportive of our relationship. Anthony put his hand on my leg, calming me down. He could feel the tremble and he looked over at me, "they will love you, baby. You have nothing to be worried about. I talk about you so much my dad probably loves you already."

When we pulled up, the house was adorable. It was the cutest ranch style house I'd ever seen. It was exactly the house I would have seen Anthony growing up in.

"So, this is the house you spent your childhood in?"

"Yep. Well, it's been through a remodel; I helped my dad a few years back with doing some touch ups to the inside and out; we re-did his kitchen, put hardwood through the house, upgraded his bathroom. Stuff like that. Now he loves it. But it was the first thing he bought all on his own for me and him, and he vowed to keep it; and one day he said it would be mine. His pride and joy;

outside of me of course," he laughed a little. I watched Anthony as he looked at the house. I could watch the movie play in his head of all the memories he had in that house. I could only imagine the times he shared in the house with his father. The good times, and maybe even the bad.

I took a slow, deep breath. I was visibly nervous. I wanted to put on a brave face, but I wanted to impress Anthony's parents. I know he held his father in a high regard, and his opinion mattered very much; so if his father didn't like me, I felt like I wouldn't be around much longer. I couldn't blame him. Based on what he went through with his mother, he needed a dependable woman in his life, and I knew that his father's approval on the woman he would share his life with meant a lot to him.

"You ready?" Anthony said. He studied my face.

"Ready."

He unlocked the door, walked over and opened my car door. When I got out, our eyes met, "don't worry babe. He will love you." He placed a small peck on my forehead.

I smiled. I needed that reassurance.

He took my hand and I took his, and we walked up the steps to his father's front door. As we were walking up, I watched the front door swing open and a tall, slender and slightly older version of Anthony opened the door with the most handsome grin on his face.

"Ant! How are you man?!"

"Hey dad!" Anthony's grin was about as big as his father's.

They both embraced one another. The hug was long. Anthony's father was a slightly darker tone than him. He had a low curly fade and a salt and pepper beard. He wore glasses that were small, so they made him look very sophisticated, but I could tell he was also a pretty rugged guy. Anthony was the spitting image of his father. When he was about 55-60, this would be exactly who he looked like.

"It's been so long. You've gotten a little taller since I saw you last, man."

"Nah old man, you've gotten shorter," Anthony laughed.

"Don't make me whoop your ass, boy."

"Not in front of my girlfriend, pop. Please."

"Ohhh, I forgot. This is the wonderful woman I've been hearing you gush about on the phone like a boy who just got his first kiss, huh?"

"Dad! What the hell, man?" Anthony said. He was blushing so hard. I thought it was cute.

"Oh my gosh! He was talking about me that much to his dad? What was he saying?!" Now my curiosity was running wild.

"Well dad, this is Chante Thomas, my girlfriend. Chante, this is my father, Randall Bishop."

I reached out my hand, "Nice to meet you Mr. Bishop."

"Girl put that hand away and come hug me," he said as he came forward and grabbed me up.

He was such a nice man. I can see where Anthony got his charm from.

"I am so happy to finally meet you. I cannot tell you how much Anthony has told me about you; I feel like I have known you forever already; like you're already my daughter."

"Oh really? Well I hope he hasn't told you too much I would have to defend."

"Oh no! I can't even let him talk bad about you now. In my

eyes, you're the perfect little angel."

I looked over at Anthony, "well looks like you're trying to gain some more brownie points, huh?"

Anthony shrugged, "I guess we'll just have to see, huh?"

Randall took my hand and escorted us both inside the house, "Anthony, you get those bags and take them in the house to the guest room. Chante, I am going to give you a tour. Did Anthony tell you we remodeled the house ourselves?"

"He did. He told me that you all made it your own little project. It looks wonderful, Mr. Bishop."

"Yea, I would take all the credit, but these old bones couldn't have done it without Ant. He is a master with his hands. I think it's just God-sent talent is all. Lord knows he didn't get it from me. I didn't know what the hell I was doing half the time. I almost called in someone to finish the stuff for me; and Anthony was just like 'nah dad, let me help."

"Yea, that sounds like Anthony. Always coming in to help. He's pretty good at that."

"Let me take you out to the deck to meet my wife, Lola."

Randall and I walked out to the deck where we met his wife, Lola, who was sitting out on a patio chair next to a table with a pitcher of lemonade and glasses waiting for us. When she heard the door open, she looked up and saw us there.

"Oh my gosh! You must be Chante! Helloooo! How are you?"

"Hi Mrs. Bishop! How are you?" I walked over and gave her a big hug. She was the sweetest woman I'd ever met. Almost as sweet as my own mother. She was so inviting and friendly.

"Randall and I have been waiting for y'all all day. Truth be told Randall hasn't been able to stop talking about you all visiting all week. He has been preparing and cleaning this house up non-stop. Even worked me to the bone, too."

"Oh hush, Lola. I wasn't that bad."

"You were insufferable, Randall; but I still love you anyway," she teased.

"Anyway baby, do you want something to drink? I got some lemonade out here?"

"I would love some, please? Can I grab some?"

"Sure!"

I went over to the table and poured myself a glass and sat down. Being on the road and in the air all day made me beat. I was happy to finally be able to sit down and relax; and Anthony's parents made that very easy to do in their home.

As I was making myself comfortable, I could hear Anthony come outside to join us.

"My parents aren't driving you nuts yet are they, sweetheart?"

"No. They were just actually about to start telling me some of the pretty embarrassing stories. So pull up a chair and come listen."

"If that's the case, I'm going back inside," Anthony said laughing.

"Not before you come give me a hug and kiss," Lola said.

"Of course!" Anthony went over to Lola and hugged her tightly. I could tell he missed her as well. She held him close and closed her eyes and whispered, "how have you been baby?"

"Good, real good mama."

"That's what I like to hear," she said.

"Well, I've got that woman over there to thank for a lot of it," I could overhear him say, as he motioned towards me. I blushed and winked at him.

Lola smiled, "you'll promise to tell me all about her?"

"I will," Anthony said.

Anthony walked over to me and gave me a kiss on the cheek. He then went to pour himself a glass of lemonade and proceed to listen to his father ramble on about the renovations he made to his deck. I was intently listening, but also admiring Anthony at the same time. I watched him as he interacted with his father, listening and laughing with him like they were old friends. I could tell that they had a very tight bond; and knowing what he went through with his mother, that the bond he shared with his father was an unbreakable one. I loved that about him and I found myself realizing that I could watch them interacting all day.

Finally, I snapped out of my trance when Lola mentioned us having dinner out on the patio. Randall was preparing the grill so we could have a small barbecue, and that some of Anthony's old friends from college were coming over.

"Anthony, we wanted to surprise you since you were coming into town. Shawn and Andrew said they haven't seen you in a few months and wanted to stop by. Is that ok?"

"Yea that's fine. They did text me the other day and said they would stop by since I was in town. So that would be great. Chante, is that cool? You get to meet a few of my friends from here?"

"I'm cool with it if you are, babe. I'm in your world so I'm down for whatever."

A few hours later, there was music playing, drinks flowing,

and food was plentiful. I had gotten comfortable at Anthony's parents' house and I was watching Anthony in his element. He was with his friends laughing and joking. I heard so many different childhood stories about him in high school and playing sports and about his past relationships, which he wasn't too proud of.

As I was sitting out on the deck, looking out at the sunset, Anthony came over and stood behind me. He placed his arms around my waist.

"How're you doing, babe?"

"I'm doing great. How are you?"

"I'm good. This feels good."

"Are you enjoying yourself?"

"I am. I really missed my boys. They are hilarious."

"They are. I'm learning so much about you that I don't think you would have told me," I said, laughing at him.

"Nah. They are definitely pulling out my old secrets."

"Your parents are the sweetest people ever, babe. I hope they like me."

"Well, a little birdie told me that you are the sweetest woman ever. And my stepmother told me that if I don't marry you, then she will personally come all the way to LA and whoop my ass. So, I guess that means I need to put a ring on it eventually," he said.

I looked back at him, "so you trying to marry me, Anthony?"

"I don't know. Depends on if I want my mama to whoop my ass or not."

I rolled my eyes and looked away. He laughed.

We watched the sunset together, his body close to mine. It was a perfect moment with a perfect man. I couldn't ask for anything else right at that moment.

In a few days, it was time for us to go. I hated to leave, because Randall and Lola had made this feel like a second home without even trying that hard.

"Now Chante, you better make sure you come and visit me without this big head boy, ok?"

"I sure will Mr. Bishop. I think me and you need to hang out some more and you can tell me some more secrets."

"Trust me, I have millions of them."

I gave him a big hug and a kiss on the cheek. I promised that I would come back to visit the next time I was in town for work. I also gave Lola a hug and kiss as well.

As I was walking to the car, I overheard Anthony and his dad talking.

"Treat her well, Ant. She's an amazing woman."

"I am dad. She's the best thing that ever happened to me, seriously."

"Well then you treat her like that, then."

My heart melted. I knew right then, I wanted to spend the rest of my life with Anthony Bishop. I hope he wanted to spend the rest of his life with me, too.

TWENTY

As the Christmas holiday had come and gone, Anthony and I prepared for New Year's. Since he was already on the East Coast, he decided to stay through the New Year and celebrate with Chelsea and I. This was the first night that I actually didn't want to be out partying. I decided to call Nia and Tara and have them bring Mariya and Josh over and we have a small little house party. They were down for it, so we bought champagne, food and on New Year's Eve, we had our own little kickback. When the clock struck midnight, I couldn't think of any place I'd rather be than to be with my friends, my daughter and the love of my life.

Shortly after we entered the new year, while I was spending a Saturday working on some newly submitted manuscripts that were coming very close to deadline, I received a shocking phone call from the last person I'd want to talk to. I immediately felt a tension headache mounting between my eyes as I proceeded to pick up my phone.

"Hello?" I said.

"Chante? I need to talk to you." It was Liyah.

I rolled my eyes and let out a long, deep sigh. "What is it, Liyah?"

"I don't need all the attitude, Chante."

"Well pardon my obvious surprise. You're not someone I talk to on the regular, nor are you someone I would be expecting a phone call from. What do you need?"

"Whatever, Chante. I should be pissed at you right now."

Liyah's tone was laced with unnecessary venom and I could not understand why; but knowing Liyah, it could be anything.

"Chante, I thought we had gotten past this petty nonsense, and I thought you had grown up; but I see you are still playing your spiteful games."

I looked at my phone like she was crazy, "Liyah, what are you talking about?"

"Don't play dumb with me. I know you are dating some guy named Anthony. What I don't believe is you are continuing to cheat on men, and of all people, why you would bring *my man* back into your drama! You just couldn't leave us alone and let us be happy, could you? I knew it would only be a matter of time before you sought your revenge, but you won't play me, bitch!'"

I wish Liyah could have seen my face when she said that, because I was completely lost on what she was talking about.

"Liyah, what the hell are you talking about?! Are you high or something? You started smoking again? I'm not cheating on Anthony with Trey. Where is all this even coming from?"

"Chante, there is no need to lie to me; I am trying to resolve this in a mature way. I don't know what's been going on between you and Trey, but it needs to stop. What's done is done and he is with *me* now. You really need to just quit while you're ahead and be happy with ONE man."

"Liyah, I really do not know what kind of game you're playing, but I haven't spoken to Trey since Christmas when I introduced him to Anthony. We really haven't had much to discuss except when he was going to pick up Chelsea for Spring Break."

I heard a long pause from Liyah as she tried to process what I was telling her. Despite our non-existent communication, I had known this woman all my life, and I knew when she knew she was dead wrong. Apparently, something was going on with Trey and she assumed that he was being distant with her, and cozying up to me. Little did she know, I learned my lesson; and now that I have Anthony, I knew that a relationship with Trey is completely out of the question.

"Chante, I am going to say this one time. You can try and tell me you're not seeing Trey on the side or anything like that, but I am not stupid. Remember, I was covering for you when you were cheating on Trey. Just be happy with your man and let me be happy with mine. Trey doesn't want you anymore, so stop trying to steal him back from me," she said.

"This bitch is delusional," I thought. "Liyah, again, I don't know what you're talking about, but you might need to slow up before you get your feelings hurt. I am not talking to Trey about anything outside of our daughter. So whoever he's cheating on you with, you need to know it's not me."

Then, I hung up the phone. Liyah tried to call me back to back about five times, but I didn't answer. I set up my phone to block her number after I received a text message stating the following:

This isn't over, bitch. We'll see who has the last laugh.

I didn't have time to think about Liyah and her drama, because I had an important topic to discuss with Anthony. We needed to discuss him moving here to stay permanently. I didn't know if we were that far along in our relationship to be making this decision, but one thing I did know is that I loved Anthony and wanted him in my life daily. The only way to do that, is for him to move in with me.

I called him that day to approach the topic with him.

"Hey baby. How are you?'

I could hear the smile in Anthony's voice, "well, this is a surprise. Phone sex in the middle of the day? You nasty girl."

"Anthony, you are nasty and that is not why I called," I said laughing.

"Ok, ok! Well, if you aren't calling to give me a midday quickie to get me through the second half of my shift, what you want, woman?" he said chuckling.

"I actually wanted to have a serious conversation with you about us."

"Are you breaking up with me?" he asked.

"Hell no! Nothing like that, but I did want to talk to you about possibly moving to the next phase in our relationship."

"I'm listening."

"Well, how would you feel about moving back to the east coast?"

There was a long pause, and a sigh. *"shit. He doesn't want to move. I'm going to have to go to California. My mother would flip her shit if she knew."*

I quickly tried to change the soften the blow, "I mean, you don't have to. We can talk about maybe me moving there, or maybe we can find somewhere in the middle so it's equal for both of us..."

"Chante, chill baby. I'm not mad, I'm thinking how mad at you I am for not letting me ask you if we could move in together," he said.

I smiled. "So, you're ok with moving here to DC?"

"Actually, yes. I've been thinking about it for some time. Ever since I came and saw Chelsea. You all have such an established life there. Chelsea has friends, she is in school. Plus, as a man, I would never want Trey to be that far from his daughter. I'm sure one day distance will be a factor, but right now,

I have nothing to truly uproot here except a job; any my firm can place me anywhere. I've been snooping around, and they have an office in DC. It would actually be the perfect move for me."

I could not believe that he was already thinking about this before I could even bring it up. He is a man that is so full of surprises sometimes I can't even take it. After we talked a little while longer about it, I had to get back to work, so I told him I would call him later that night so we could really discuss what the timeline would be for him moving. He agreed.

When I hung up the phone, I felt more at peace with the way my life was headed at this time. Everything seemed to be flowing so effortlessly between Anthony and I. The easier it became, the easier it was for me to fall deeper and deeper in love with this man.

When I got home that evening, before I called Anthony again, I sat down with Chelsea to discuss with her what could be a big shift in her life. I wanted to make sure that before anything, my daughter would be ok with this process.

"Baby girl, I need to ask you a question; and I need you to be honest."

"What's up mommy?" Chelsea said. She was sounding more and more grown up every day.

"What if Mr. Anthony came to stay with us for good? How would you feel about that?"

She looked into the sky as if she was giving it some thought. After about thirty seconds (that almost killed me in suspense), she finally said, "I think I would like it. I like Mr. Anthony! I always hate when he has to leave and we can't hang out anymore."

I was able to breathe again, "good, because mommy and Mr. Anthony have been talking about him possibly coming to live here permanently. It looks like Mommy and Mr. Anthony will be together for a very long time."

Nia was at my house one Saturday, doing our usual; day drinking champagne and catching up on all the shows we never watch during the week. We ordered pizza and wings and ate horribly all day. It had become sort of a ritual of ours, something to look forward to when we had a shitty week. Lately, my life had been pretty good, and I hadn't gotten to share all the latest details with Nia. Today was the perfect day for us to catch up.

"She did WHAT?!" Nia said as she poured her third glass of champagne. She was already on a four, if we're scaling 1-10.

"She accused me of still talking to Trey; scheming with him or something. But she is wrong, because I don't want anything to do, nor do I desire to have anything to do with Trey. We are finally cordial and I'm not trying to ruin that, especially now that Chelsea can see her parents being civil towards one another."

"Exactly. This Liyah bitch is something else. Tara was telling me some stuff about her. She's crazy as hell."

"She truly is. Sadly though, sometimes I miss her."

Nia looked at me with a weird face, "really? The woman who fucked your husband and got pregnant?"

I laughed, "well, not that part of her. The part that I had grown to love; the part that was like my sister. Liyah was so much fun to be around. If she wasn't such a bitch now, you'd probably love her because she was always the life of our little party. She pushed me out of my comfort zone and made me somewhat of who I am today. So, yea, sometimes I miss the friendship we had, and I wish she valued it enough to cherish it."

"That's crazy Chante. She did not have to do you like that."

"Exactly. I would have been able to forgive her if she had

even snitched on me to Trey, instead of sleeping with him."

I had finally told Nia the whole sordid ordeal between Trey, Liyah and I a while back. She didn't really judge me for it and was more pissed at Liyah and what she did than what I did. I had honestly thought that Tara had given her more details than I had (you know, about the whole me screwing Tara's husband thing), but she never mentioned it to me. Maybe Nia knew that there were some things that were best left unsaid, or maybe Tara never told her either. No matter what the reason, Nia let me tell as much as the situation as I was comfortable with, and I could appreciate that. And I felt like eventually, my past may come to haunt me, so I needed her to know something about it.

"Well, enough about your whoreish past," Nia said, smirking at me. I threw my couch pillow at her and grabbed a slice of pizza, "What's going on in your future? How is Mr. Anthony doing?"

Just hearing his name made my heart flutter and I smiled like a sixth grader with a huge crush, "he's doing great actually. I love being around him, I love the way he makes me feel....ugh! I just love him!"

"Ooo girl, yea, you're in love. All that corny cheesy grinning and shit; you're definitely in love."

"Whatever. I'm sure you feel that way about Tara."

"I don't know if I'm that deep in love yet, but I definitely love her. She's amazing. She's on my mind every day and every time I see her, I'm at peace. I didn't know love could really be like this. Now that she's here in DC permanently, it gives me the opportunity to be around her more, get to know more of her. I never thought I could feel this way about anyone."

I was happy to hear Nia happy, and especially to know Tara is happy. Tara had been through so much, partly as me to blame; and I wanted her to be happy. I'm glad that she was able to find some peace by being with Nia.

I had gotten so lost in the happy thoughts of Tara and Nia being a happy couple, I almost didn't hear the question Nia asked me.

"Wait, what did you say?"

"So, when do you think he's going to pop the question, Chante? Hell, he's not my man and even I've been waiting, shit!" Nia said, as she was sitting on my couch, looking through some of her latest photos in the portfolio she brought over.

"Girl, that's not even something that's on the radar right now. I don't think I'm ready for all that to be honest," I said. I was in the kitchen pouring our last bottle of champagne for the day. At some point, we had to stop because we had to go get the girls from their play date. Nia was very flattering, but little did she know, I didn't know if marriage was really where I was at, at this point. I was simply enjoying Anthony's company, and although our relationship was pretty serious, I was convinced that the idea of him wanting to marry me is a long way off. Moving in was big enough right now.

Nia continued to root for marriage in my favor, though. "I don't know what you're talking about. I can see the way Anthony looks at you, the way he treats you; he is a man in love, and he plans on putting a ring on it; watch what I tell you, sis," she said. I rolled my eyes at her as I walked into the room with our glasses and an open bottle. She took mine from me and winked at me.

"Anyways, enough discussion about me and my man. What are you working on over there?" I said as I sat next to her on the couch. By now, all of our shows had ended, and I had the television on, but we weren't really watching.

"Just picking out the final prints from a shoot I did last week. I think they came out really good, what do you think?"

I looked over her shoulder as she studied the prints. They

really did look amazing. I never doubted that Nia was an amazing photographer. She was one of the best I had ever seen. My mind began to wander to how engagement pictures would look if Anthony and I took them. I imagined us being in my favorite park; smiling, laughing and enjoying the fact that we were in love. I would be looking into his eyes and admiring the huge rock that he would have placed on my finger and....

"Chante!" I heard Nia call out to me.

I snapped out of my trance and looked at her with a confused look, "what?!"

"Bitch, where were you? I was calling your name," Nia said laughing and sipping her drink.

"Girl, I went to another place. You mentioned engagement, and I was looking at these pictures and I have to admit, Anthony being my husband wouldn't be the worst possible thing to happen to me. I just don't know if he is truly ready to accept me for who I am, or who I was at least."

"Girl, please! I bet Anthony can look past all of that nonsense and see you for the woman you are today. I mean, you have been an amazing girlfriend to him; I don't see why he wouldn't want to marry you. The past is the past, sis. If he didn't want to forgive you, I don't think he would've gone this far into a relationship with you. I mean, meeting Chelsea, your mom? He's all in, Tae. Trust."

"Well, I guess we will see what the future holds, because I really don't know what's in his head at this point."

TWENTY-ONE

A few hours later, I had talked to Anthony, who was discussing his upcoming trip to come visit. We had been making a pretty consistent commitment to seeing one another at least as much as our relationship and lives allowed. We never wanted to put a number on how many times we *had* to see one another, we just wanted to make sure there was a joint effort. It definitely was and we had no issues with that. Anytime Anthony wanted to hop on a plane and see me, he was there and vice versa. Now that he had met Chelsea, I even let her come with me on a few visits.

Anthony was due to fly in to see me for the weekend, so the week I had at work was less than productive. I didn't want this to happen, but now that Nia had opened the "M" door, as much as I tried to not think about it, I failed miserably. All day at work, I couldn't quite get him and the idea of him being my forever out of my mind. I still was hesitant about the idea overall; I didn't think he was even thinking on that same level as I; however, Nia had a good point. Anthony appeared to be all in with me, and maybe marriage was the next step, and I was just not ready to admit it. Either way, I thought more and more that maybe this weekend would be the weekend we bring up that topic, just to see where his head was at.

That Thursday afternoon, I was at the airport waiting on him at his terminal. I was feeling especially corny this visit, with the recent marriage thoughts floating through my head, so I even made a cute sign with his name on it, decorated with hearts. As much as my mind says I'm not ready, I think my heart was singing a different tune. Plus, I hadn't seen him in a couple of weeks, and I was missing him like crazy; so, I hoped he liked my little sign, even though it wasn't much.

I stood at the terminal where I was expecting Anthony, as I did so many times the past couple of months, and just as he did for me. I watched as several other people passed by me and smiled, as they saw the sign that I had written for Anthony, which said "My king, Mr. Bishop". One man even stopped by me and said, "Mr. Bishop is a lucky man, having a beautiful woman like you waiting on him." I smiled coyly and told him thank you. I continued to wait patiently, tapping my foot and my eyes darting left and right trying to make sure I didn't miss him coming out of the tunnel.

A few seconds later, I saw him. He was dressed casually; sweatpants and a hoodie, his typical travel wear. He had on his favorite sneakers, something I learned about him, and had his headphones on, probably busting his eardrums with how loud it could possibly be. He was looking down at his phone, and when he finally looked up, our eyes locked. I couldn't tell you whose smile was wider at that moment. I could see his pace quicken with the sight of my face. I looked at him and became breathless. Before I knew it, he had swept me up in his arms and spun me around.

"Baby, put me down!" I laughed.

"No! I need this moment, because I've been wanting to do this ever since I got on the plane in LA. I've missed you, girl." He said. I was melting at every word he was saying.

"I've missed you too, boy." I looked down at him and kissed him passionately. I didn't give a damn who was watching in the airport at that moment.

Anthony put me down and grabbed his bag off the baggage claim. We interlocked fingers and walked to my car parked right outside. Even after a long flight, in true 'Anthony' fashion, he took my keys from me and insisted that he drive, because he felt that it was a "man's job to drive his woman around." It was these types of things I missed the most; the catering, the pampering and the gestures that only gentlemen can show.

As we were on our way home, I couldn't help but be nervous in anticipation of our night ahead. Nia had agreed to watch Chelsea for me tonight, so that Anthony and I could have some much needed and deserved alone time. I couldn't lie, I was horny as hell and ready for a night of freaky, rough sex from my man. Right about now, I was glad I agreed for Chelsea to not be home.

When we got home, Anthony hopped in the shower to freshen up from the long day. He knew exactly where my mind was at, and he wasn't playing any games either. As he was showering, I went in my closet and pulled out the outfit I planned on wearing for him that night. I had hinted at him getting a 'new Chante' tonight, and I didn't plan to disappoint. A few minutes later, I heard my bathroom door open and I immediately hid my lingerie set under my towel. Anthony walked out of the shower with just his towel on. I swear if it wasn't for self-control, I would have taken him right then. I had to calm myself down, though. I didn't want to rush the evening.

Anthony noticed me staring at his half-naked body and said, "you see something you like?"

"No." I said sarcastically.

"Yea, ok. I see you staring at me. You need to watch out before your eyes get stuck like that; all bugged out and stuff." He said as he made an exaggerative face as to assume that is how I looked at him.

"Whatever, Anthony. Are you finished in the bathroom? I need to freshen up for tonight."

"Yes ma'am. I'll be out here waiting on you, love."

"Ok." I said. I walked over and kissed him on the lips lightly, "there is a bottle of wine on chill in the fridge. Open it and bring it in the bedroom. Pour yourself a glass, and I will pour one when I get out."

"I am liking the sound of this already." He said. He went into the kitchen and I walked into the bathroom.

I took a quick but satisfying shower and began to moisturize my entire body. I began to put on my lingerie for the evening, tussle my hair a bit and put on a fresh coat of lipstick. I had on a red laced corset and thong set, with 2 thigh garters. My titties were sitting up pretty high, and my body was glistening from the moisturizer I used. *"yea, he won't be able to resist me tonight."* I said to myself. I took one last look at myself in the mirror, admired the view and then proceeded to make my way into the bedroom for our nightcap.

TWENTY-TWO

When Anthony saw me, he could barely say a word. He took a good minute examining every inch of my frame, licking his lips in the process. I decided to play him at his own games.

"Do you see something you like?"

"Oh, definitely. You look absolutely beautiful, baby."

"Thank you, Ant. I have been waiting for this night for a while now, so I wanted to impress you; you like?" I asked. I was feeling confident, but deep down I was a little nervous on if he was going to like it. Nia was with me when I bought the lingerie, and she guaranteed that this would get me laid within minutes. I hope she was right.

"Baby, I more than like this. I love this. Come sit with me for a minute and I will show you how much I enjoy seeing you like this," Anthony said.

I walked over to him slowly and allowed him to wrap me up in his arms. The way he enveloped me in his embrace brought heat to every part of my body. He let his lips brush against my breast before placing soft kisses on each one. I looked down at him and we kissed. He got into it and began to reach up and massage my scalp as he returned the passion in his kiss.

Anthony proceeded to lay me down into the bed and I stopped him, "No, no no... I am in control tonight, sir," I said. I sat up and straddled his waist. I continued to plant soft, sensual kisses on his neck, shoulders and chest. He moaned as I continued to make my way down his body. As I moved further and further, he stopped me.

He pulled me closer to his face and kissed me. He looked me in the eye as he grabbed my hips and navigated them towards his throbbing manhood. I eased slowly down on top of him, moving up and down in a slow, winding rhythm. We looked each other in the eye, our breath rising and falling. I grabbed ahold of his shoulders and continued to roll and gyrate on top of him. He put his hands around my waist and made sure to maintain the same level of intensity I was giving him. I didn't want to stop. I wanted to make love to him all night long, and I could tell he wanted to do the same.

He sat up straight and kissed my neck, gradually moving towards sucking my breast, that sat perky and erect in his face. He cupped both with each hand as he licked and sucked each one with intensity. He was still holding onto my waist when he flipped me over and lay me on the bed. He gripped the sheet above my head and stroked me. I could see the lust in his eyes he had for me. He stroked and stroked, panting heavily with each thrust of passion until he reached his climax.

The next morning, I woke up with Anthony still holding me at my waist. My back was facing him, and I could feel his nose buried in the corner of my neck. I felt like I was hungover, but when I noticed that we did not even make it through our bottle of wine, I knew I was drunk from the love making that went down the night before. A smile ran across my lips just thinking of it. I turned over, and faced Anthony to watch him sleep. He stirred a little when I moved, but he made sure that I never left his arms. I kissed him lightly on his forehead and listened to his breath as he slept. I watched him sleep until sleep found me again, and I fell asleep again.

When I woke up a second time, I was in the bed by myself. I woke up and looked around the room to see if Anthony was there. He wasn't. I called out his name and did not hear anyone answer back, so I went for my phone to text him. When I opened my phone, I saw a text message waiting on me. It was from Anthony:

"Hey babe, I went to that bakery that you love so much to grab the sweetest and unhealthiest doughnut I could find. I'll bring you one too and some coffee. Love you."

The man truly knew the way to my heart. I decided to get up and straighten up my room, which looked like the scene in a college apartment the morning after a lot of liquor and sex. Articles of clothes and towels were everywhere, and at least three condom wrappers. The good thing was Chelsea was not here to see her mother be ratchet. I went to the bathroom and took a quick shower, threw on my old college sweatshirt and some shorts, and made my way to my office. I decided that since Anthony was out, I will get some writing done for the morning. I plugged my iPhone up to my speakers, lit my favorite candle and sat down on my chaise lounge and pulled my MacBook out.

I was deep into the writing zone when I heard Anthony come back to the house. I didn't even realize that he was looking at me in my doorway, holding a box full of doughnuts and my coffee.

I looked up and suddenly snapped out of my trance, "Hey baby! I'm sorry, let me get that," I jumped up and walked over to him to grab my coffee. "I didn't even notice you there, you know when I start writing I get locked in and can't stop."

"Trust me, I know," He said. "I kind of enjoy watching your creative process, though. It's very intriguing."

"What a compliment. You must be gunning for extra points here, Mr. Bishop."

"I hope I have all the points I need, love. I just want to make you as happy as you make me every day."

"Well, you don't do a bad job at that, babe." I grabbed a doughnut out of the box and kissed him on the cheek. When I looked down into the box, I almost dropped my coffee.

I didn't want to ask such a stupid question, but I wanted to make sure my eyes weren't playing tricks on me, "Anthony, baby; what is that in the bottom of this box?"

Anthony looked in the box and casually looked up at me, flashing his signature smile, "I don't know, but it looks like a ring box to me."

Anthony put the box down on my end table, took the small black box out of the doughnut box and took my hand.

"Sit down, Chante Thomas. I have something very important I would like to say to you."

I wasn't sure if my feet even moved; I was certain I flew over to my chair. I sat down and watched Anthony slowly get down on one knee and open the ring box. I was speechless. The ring was flawless. My mouth dropped so far open I could have tripped over my bottom lip.

"Chante, ever since we laid eyes on each other, I knew fate had brought us back into each other's circle. Since that date, I have been able to get to know you and see how beautiful your soul is. I know you are an amazing woman, a woman I need in my life to make me better. I love you to the ends of this earth, and if I could go any further, I would love you that entire distance as well. Chante Thomas, I want you to be my wife. Will you marry me?"

I couldn't fight back the tears. I couldn't describe the feeling that had come over me in that moment. It was like he shot a drug through my bloodstream. I couldn't believe that he was asking me to marry him. I couldn't believe he wanted me, despite all my flaws and the shit I did in my past, he still wanted me to be his wife. He was giving me the second chance to be a great wife. I had to ask him, before I made my decision, I had to ask him.

"Anthony, are you sure? Are you sure you want me after the things I have done in my past?"

"Yes. Because I don't care about your past. I care about how you persevered through that. I care about what you have learned from that experience and the promise that you will make to me to never do that again. I trust that you deserve a second chance at love. Give me the opportunity to let you have that chance and let me have the honor of being your husband."

"Ok. Yes! I will marry you!" I said through tears. He placed the ring on my finger, and I fell into his arms.

Happily ever after *does* happen twice in one lifetime.

The plan was to pick up Chelsea later on that afternoon, but I couldn't think straight. I could not believe what had happened. Anthony and I spent the rest of the morning making passionate "we just got engaged" sex all through the apartment, and about three hours later, we were laying in my bed, re-watching a movie that we tried to watch once before, but both fell asleep. I was laying on his chest and Anthony was caressing my back as we looked at the TV.

"So, how does it feel?" he said.

"What do you mean?"

"The ring. How does it feel to want to be fully committed to me for the rest of your old days?" he chuckled.

"Honestly, I cannot describe it. I never thought I'd have a second chance to fall in love; let alone, be someone's wife. I thought I had tainted those opportunities long ago when Trey and I divorced."

"Well, I cannot tell you how happy you've made me, Chante. Ever since that day we saw one another in LA, I haven't been able to get you out of my mind. I thought a second chance at love was too good for me too, but you made it happen for me. I will love you forever for that."

My first call was to my mother. I didn't even know what to say, so when she answered, all I said was, "I'm getting married!"

"Wait, what?"

"I'm getting...married?" I said again. I couldn't tell if she was shocked, upset or both.

"Oh, my goodness Chante! Are you for real? Anthony.... proposed?" By the tone of her voice, I decided to get up and take our conversation to another room.

"Yes mama, he did this morning. You don't sound very excited for me."

"No baby, it's not that. I just.... well it's so soon. How well do you know Anthony, and is he serious? I mean any man can put a ring on it just to keep reaping the benefits of a good woman."

"Mom, I think I'm fine. He is serious. I know him; Anthony is not going to just shell out this kind of money for a ring and not be serious."

I heard a long pause; one that shocked me as I thought my mother would be happy for me. Oddly, that was not the feeling I was getting from this call.

"Well, if he's serious, then I guess I can accept that. It's just so new Chante. I don't even really know this guy like I knew Trey. Trey would come over and hang out all the time."

"The difference between that is that Anthony is on the West Coast. He doesn't have the luxury of coming to visit you. But trust me, he does want to get to know you more, and when you guys met at Christmas you looked thrilled to meet him."

"It's definitely going to take some getting used to, but if you love him Chante, and Chelsea loves him, then I'm in. I'm happy for you baby, always will be."

I ended the call with my mother, and although her apprehension was a little unsettling, I took it in stride. I knew that eventually she will grow to love Anthony; she just had to get Trey out of her system.

Later that day, I went to pick up Chelsea, and I was nervous about giving her the news. Having Anthony around only as "mommy's friend" was one thing; I didn't know how she would react when she found out that we would be getting married.

When I arrived at Nia's house to pick her up, she noticed my ring from a mile away when she opened the door. She jumped up and down grinning like a child who just got a shiny new bike for Christmas.

"Oh. My. God. GIRL! That ring is HUGE! I told you, I told you, I told you he was going to propose!!! I'm so happy for you," she yelled as I ran up to her and gave her a hug.

"Yea, I still can't believe it myself. He asked me this morning. I was tore up too, girl. Just got out of bed in his T-shirt looking a mess. But he loves me and the mess that I am I guess."

"I'm so happy for you, Chante. You want me to call Chelsea?"

"Yes. I have to tell her; I don't know how she will take it though."

Nia called Chelsea's name and I could hear her running down the hall. She saw me and jumped into my arms.

"Hi mommy! I missed you!"

"Hi baby. I've missed you too. Did you have fun with Mariya?"

"I did. But I'm ready to come home. I have to get ready for school."

"That's right," I laughed. She was way too intelligent for her own six-year-old mind to handle.

While Chelsea was putting on her shoes, I decided to spill the beans, the suspense was killing me.

"Baby, I want to tell you something important."

"what mommy?"

"Well, you remember how I told you that I really liked Mr. Anthony, but he wasn't your new dad just yet?"

"Yea..."

"Well today, Mr. Anthony asked me to marry him. And I said yes."

Her eyes lit up, "Really? Awwww mommy!"

My heart melted more than when Anthony asked me to marry him just hours ago. Her ability to find the joy and happiness in every little thing is what keeps me lifted. She was so excited for a milestone in a relationship that she didn't understand; she just knew that if I was happy, it had to be a good thing. And Anthony was my good thing.

"We have to hurry home; I want him to be able to tell you some details as well."

Chelsea put on her shoes, hugged Nia and yelled good-bye to Mariya. She wanted to get home as soon as possible to hear the news.

About twenty minutes later, we were home. Anthony was watching TV in the living room when we arrived.

"Hi Mr. Anthony!" Chelsea said as she walked in.

"Well hello sweetheart! How are you?"

"Great! Mommy is getting married!" she jumped and squealed in excitement.

Anthony laughed a hearty laugh, "well is that so? Well in that case there is a very important conversation you and I need to have. Come sit down next to me."

Chelsea obliged him after she took off her shoes and jacket.

"Now, I have been here in your mom's life for a long time now. And I feel closer and closer to you and your mother every day. You guys are a very important part of my life and I wanted to know; since we are so close, can I be your bonus dad?"

The tears didn't stop flowing. To hear Anthony have such undoubted feelings for Chelsea, a child that is not biologically his but loves her like his own, was too much for me to bear. Even when I thought I knew all the ways to charm me, he pulls one out of nowhere.

TWENTY-THREE

I sat at work daydreaming and staring at my left hand. It felt good to see something on my ring finger again. I couldn't stop smiling. Everyone in my office couldn't' help but stop by my door and congratulate me. I just held my cheesy grin, while telling everyone thank you. Anthony text me as I was scrolling through emails, attempting to act as if I was working.

"Stop looking at that ring and get to work, future Mrs. Bishop."

A faint smile filled my face as I grabbed my phone to text him back.

"Well, if the ring wasn't so distracting, I wouldn't be so unfocused at work."

"I couldn't dare get you a ring any smaller than that, and it doesn't even begin to represent how much I love you."

"Oh stop it Ms. Thomas, you're making us all jealous," my assistant said. Apparently, my smile was radiating in all parts of my office.

"Sorry girl, I am just so happy. I haven't felt this in love since I was with Trey."

For a minute, I had a split-second flashback moment. I remember the feeling I felt almost ten years ago, when Trey popped the question. It was more formal than the latter, but with Anthony, I didn't care where I was or what I was doing. In that moment, we were just us, a man in love with a woman who asked for her hand in marriage. Anthony and I were going to be great together; there was no doubt in my mind

In my mid-thoughts about Trey, I realized he does not know of my most recent news. I knew that I was due to drive Chelsea down to meet with him soon, and I wouldn't want him to find out from her that way. I wanted to be up front with him and let him know what was going on and that Anthony would indeed be a more permanent part of mine and Chelsea's life.

I picked up my phone, hesitant and reluctant to dial. I knew what needed to be done, despite me wanting to actually do it. His phone rang and rang, until he answered, just as I was about to give up and hang up.

"Hey Chante."

"Hello Trey. How are you?"

"Fine."

There was an awkward pause. I didn't know how to say it, what to say or how to approach it. So, I just dived in head first.

"I just wanted to tell you something; I guess I felt like I needed to make you aware of this; it's something that's going to affect Chelsea."

"O.... k? Is everything ok?"

"Yes. Everything is fine. Anthony asked me to marry him, and I said yes. So, I'll be getting married."

This was Trey's turn to insert the pause. It felt as if time froze for just a few moments. I didn't know his next move, or what his response would be.

"Wow. Um, congratulations I guess."

"Ok, thanks. Like I said I wanted you to know because this means Anthony will be around Chelsea a lot more. He will be moving here permanently in a couple weeks."

"When are y'all getting married? I hope not that soon."

I wish Trey could have seen the face I made. "That seemed a little harsh. Why exactly would it matter?"

"Well I mean Chante, you've only known this man for what, a year? Seems a little fast to me, but it's your life."

"Trey, I only told you out of the respect for Chelsea. I thought I was being the mature one by letting you know another man will be in her life. One she can willingly work towards calling her stepfather. I thought that you would want to know that, instead of making this all about when I'm getting married, how long I've been with Anthony and when we're moving in together. Truth be told, it's none of your business and you're the last person to judge my relationship choice."

"No need to be hostile Chante. I mean, who am I to judge you, right? I just find it a little...quick, to be jumping right back into a marriage so soon. I mean, have you learned from your past?"

"You can go to hell, Trey. You and Liyah are the only ones who continue to hold on to that. Y'all have moved on and minded your business and I don't throw it in your face. How about this be the last time we speak about my personal affairs. Just know, your daughter will have a stepfather; a damn good one... Oh, and tell Liyah to stop calling me, ok? Thanks!"

I hung up. I was fuming. Trey had completely taken the joy away from me that I had. Why was he so hell-bent on making my life hell and continuing to bring up the oldest shit? It didn't make sense, and it was getting on my nerves. I told myself that I would promise to keep him further and further out of my business, unless it had to do with Chelsea. That was my last time being nice.

"Forget about him Chante. I respect what you were doing, but honestly, he doesn't seem to deserve your respect," Anthony said as we lay in bed together. He was stroking my hair, my favorite thing for him to do as I watched TV.

"I know, but I wish he would just stop throwing our past in my face. I mean I get it, I screwed up; but that doesn't mean I can't change, and it doesn't mean I can't be loved or fall in love again. He did, but I'm supposed to be alone forever?!"

"Do you think he's jealous?"

"Jealous?! Of what?"

"Of the fact that you moved on, and you didn't choose him again."

I thought about it. It was a very far-fetched idea to me; to think that Trey would actually want me back. I doubted it highly, but Anthony seemed to think that maybe that's where his pent-up negativity was coming from. To be honest, it could explain his petty nature, but I don't know.

"I don't know exactly. I mean, it's shocking that I even said this much to him on the phone. But it could be true. I have no idea, and I honestly don't care."

Anthony burrowed himself further and further under my comforter, and turned off the light, "well, it's a mystery for another day. All I know is, it doesn't need to bother us any further."

He was right, I had allowed that to take up too much of my day. My frustration with Trey always seems to get the better of me, because I just want to move forward, and stop moving backwards so much. I don't care if Trey is miserable, it doesn't mean he has to bring me down with him.

TWENTY-FOUR

After the initial excitement of engagement wore off, Anthony and I were in full planning mode. We decided that we did not want to have a very long engagement, so we planned to get married in about six months; which left me virtually little room for error in planning our ceremony. The way he put it, "when you know, you know. Why have a long engagement when I know I want to spend the rest of my life with you?" With that mentality, I began to prepare for our happily ever after.

We had decided that after he moved down here and we got married, we would continue to look for a bigger place. Since I was currently living in DC, he wanted to find a house in a more suburban part of the DMV area. Once he locked in his transfer at his job, there was nothing holding him back. He has his storage set up and had all his things relocated to the East Coast. The last time he was due to fly in, I took Chelsea with me and we both surprised him. I was so excited that this was the last time we would have to catch flights to see one another. Now I would come home every day and he would be there.

When he got to the airport, Chelsea and I were waiting. When he walked through the terminal for the final time, it started to feel more permanent. We locked eyes and I knew that this man was truly going to be my forever. I was so excited I could barely contain myself.

"Hello beautiful," he said as he met me face to face.

"Hello," I said.

We were finally together, and he never had to leave again.

On the marriage planning front, I naturally chose Nia and Tara to be by my side at my wedding. Tara was very happy and honored, as I was that she accepted my invitation. Anthony and I decided that we did not want a huge wedding, so everything would be very small, elegant and private. With the news of me being engaged already blowing up on social media, I didn't want any other parts of the process to be broadcast by the media.

Nia wasted no time getting into planning mode for what she described "the best night of my second single life." She and Tara, who were chosen to be my bridesmaids, were planning my bachelorette party. They would not tell me a thing, except that it would be a very elegant, yet ratchet affair. Nia, Tara and I were all at her house, talking and planning away.

"Can you at least tell me when this is happening? I need to make sure I can be off work."

"Chante don't play that. You're the boss. You can be off whenever you want. Plus, you have your cell phone glued to you all damn day, so I'm sure you will be checking into the office whenever you want," Tara said.

I guess Tara was right. It's not like I couldn't take time off at a moment's notice; I just wanted to be nosey and find out what was going on.

"So, did you tell Trey you were getting married?" Nia asked.

"Yes. That went…. as well as I could imagine it would go."

"I bet Liyah is going to have fun with that, based on what you've been telling me about her," Tara said. She and I had some time to catch up recently, so she was privy to all of my drama with Liyah. She couldn't believe that someone who married *my* ex, someone who was supposedly my sister, could be so bitter, upset and angry still after two years. I couldn't believe it myself, but I figured she was just being spiteful and bitchy; which at this point was draining and I wanted no part of it.

We got back on track, and as Nia wrapped up whatever she was researching on her laptop about my bachelorette party, she shifted gears towards my engagement party.

"So, now we can talk about the things that you can participate in. How many guests are you anticipating for your engagement party?"

"Honestly, I didn't know if I really wanted to have a party. I mean, I had one for my first marriage, I don't know if I'm really in the mood to have another."

Nia and Tara both looked at me with a shocking facial expression.

"Girl, we are going to have a party. You deserve to celebrate the new love you have found in your life. And you deserve to show it off to everyone! Plus, I've already selected a venue and a caterer, so you're going to have to get me a guest list together," Nia said.

I smiled at her. I couldn't believe she was going through all this trouble, but I had to appreciate it. Years ago, this was Liyah, being there as my best friend and maid of honor. It did hurt a little to know we will never be in that place ever again, but I will survive.

TWENTY-FIVE

When I got home from work, Anthony was making dinner. My place smelled wonderful. I looked around to my kitchen and saw Anthony hard at work, putting our meal together over a hot stove. It made my heart melt.

I walked over to him in the kitchen and gave him a kiss, "hey baby! It smells amazing in here, what are you cooking?"

"Lamb chops, vegetables and rice. I know Trey is a chef, but I'd like to think I can throw down in the kitchen as well," he said. I smiled at him and enjoyed the wonderful aroma coming from my kitchen.

"You're better," I said.

A few minutes later, when I came back from my bedroom after changing clothes, Anthony asked me a startling question.

"Hey babe, guess what happened today?" Anthony asked me.

By now I was near the bar, pouring a glass of wine. "what happened?"

"Liyah sent me some messages about how you're some no-good chick and that I shouldn't even be messing with you, and doesn't see how I could possibly want to marry you after what you did in the past to your ex. Why would she do that?"

I can't even believe she found you on Facebook. What did she say I did this time?"

"She didn't say anything because I didn't respond. I

figured it was some drama, and you know how I feel about drama. So, I didn't respond. I wanted to talk to you about it first, see if there was anything I needed to know?" he said.

"I'm going to tell you the truth, because I don't want any more secrets. She actually called me a few weeks ago, accusing me of still having contact with Trey, when she knows I only talk to Trey about Chelsea. Lately she's been so paranoid, she's usually right up under his ass when I talk to him, I can hear her in the background. I've never had a conversation with Trey without hearing her on the phone. Even when Chelsea is with me and he Facetimes her, she is right there. After that phone call with Liyah went down, I left it alone. I mean, I still talk to Trey obviously because of Chelsea; but it is very brief because I don't need that shit in my life."

"Well, I almost let her ass have it; talking about my fiancé like that. But I guess I can see your point. We not entertaining all that bullshit baby. You know I don't play those games."

I walked up to him and kissed him on the lips to quiet him, "Ant, do you see me worried or concerned? Liyah is an afterthought. I don't know how old she thinks we are, but I am big girl and I am not playing games. Don't worry. I'll handle it tonight. You won't hear from her again."

"Uh oh. You not about to fight her, are you?"

"She is all the way in Miami and wouldn't even be worth the flight. Don't worry, I'll handle it like a lady," I said with a wink.

I kissed him again, sipped my wine and went to my bedroom.

"Let me know when dinner is done baby, I can't wait to taste it."

I walked right into my room and pulled out my phone. I called Liyah so I could set her ass straight. She answered as soon as it rung.

"Listen bitch, you're about to piss me the fuck off. I have moved on with my life and you have too. Continuing to try and sabotage my relationship with my fiancé is not going to change that I don't give a damn about you or Trey unless in concerns Chelsea. He knows about everything, so there is nothing you're telling him that he doesn't already know."

"He's actually marrying you after the shit you pulled? Hell, you must be one lucky bitch."

She was drunk. I could tell by the slur in her voice.

"Liyah, I'm not even going to argue with you, because, you're not worth it. My man is cooking me a hot meal after my long ass day at work, so here's what I'm going to do. You and Trey go do whatever it is y'all do, while Anthony, Chelsea and I have a wonderful dinner, my man rubs my feet, fucks me silly and I fall sound asleep knowing I am happy and you're miserable trying to ruin my life; someone who frankly doesn't give a damn about you."

"Bragging about your life doesn't make me feel bad, bitch. You need to watch yourself. I know exactly how to ruin that perfect little life you think you have. I know shit you don't know I'm aware of."

Click.

That's what I heard next. I rolled my eyes and put my phone on the charger. I had no idea what the hell Liyah was concocting, but I wanted no part of it. Before I left my bedroom, I sent Trey a text. I was sick of Liyah and her bullshit and I wanted to make sure I sent a warning to him; that I wasn't going to play these games with the Wright household.

I understand that I may be the most hated person in you and Liyah's world right now, but I would appreciate it if Liyah left MY MAN alone. She needs to stop trying to engage him on social media. He isn't interested. We're good over here, so keep her on a leash before I handle it myself."

I hit send and put my phone back on the charger and on Do Not Disturb. I didn't even want to hear the notification if or when he texts back. I was through with them. I walked over to Chelsea's room and checked on her. I told her dinner would be ready soon. She said ok and went back to reading her book.

I walked back up to the kitchen and sat at the table. I watched Anthony as he moved around the kitchen cooking for his two ladies. He was at peace, and now, so was I.

TWENTY-SIX

Within a month, Tara, Nia and I boarded a plan to New York City for my bachelorette party. Nia didn't tell me what was planned while we were there, but I was more than happy to have a long weekend away. Wedding planning was getting more and more stressful by the day, but no matter what, Anthony stayed positive about the entire situation. He was also getting acclimated to the area and his new position within his company. Things were overall going pretty well for us, but we were more than anxious about going ahead and jumping the broom already. So, with all that stress, I needed to have some time with my girls!

We arrived in New York early afternoon, just in time to check in early to our hotel suite for the weekend. The suite was beautiful, it was one of the nicest ones in NYC, and it was all ours for the entire weekend! Nia had told me once we got to the room, that we would be having massages in the room shortly after, so we all freshened up and prepared for their arrival. There was already complimentary champagne in the room for the occasion, so we popped the cork on bottle number one and got the party started.

The massages were the best I'd had in a long time, and after they provided us with someone to do manicures and pedicures. I sat back in my massage chair in the hotel spa, with a drink in one hand and a manicurist working on the other.

"Man, this is relaxing as hell!" I said.

Nia looked over at me, "I'm glad you're enjoying this. I'm not really the 'pamper me' type, but for you, I'm willing to do this. It's actually pretty relaxing."

"Maybe I'll treat you to it once a month if you act right,"

Tara said to her, winking at her.

Nia smiled at Tara, "I like the sound of that, babe."

"Oh stop it both of you! This weekend is about me, not y'all," I joked.

"Whatever!" Tara said.

"But honestly, I haven't had this much fun since.... well, since we went to Miami, Chante."

I almost choked on my champagne. I remembered that trip, all too well. It was the trip that I found out who Channing really was. But there were parts of that fling that Tara didn't know.

"Yea. I remember. That was a wild trip," I said in between gulps and refills of my drink.

"Dang, was it that crazy? Tara, is there anything you wanna tell me?" Nia said jokingly.

"Oh no. Just ancient history at this point," Tara said, cutting the conversation short.

"Oh...."

"Trust me, Nia. It is not important. We all have a past, and we want to keep it there," I said.

Nia nodded and understood. She didn't push it any further. I wasn't sure what all Tara told her, and I wasn't about to expose all of Tara's business, because some of it was mine too.

We moved on from the awkward and uncomfortable and proceeded with our amazing weekend. Nia pulled out all the stops for me to celebrate. We had a private five-star dinner prepared for us, a night on the town dancing, and even a morning brunch to cap off the weekend. It was the best weekend I'd had with friends in a long time, but I was more than ready to get home to Anthony and

Chelsea. The older I got, the more I realized how much I'd rather be a homebody then out partying. As we were flying back to DC, Tara had admitted the same thing.

"Girl, this weekend was the best, but I can't wait to see my little man when we get back," she said sitting next to me. Nia was across the row on a separate aisle seat asleep.

"I know right! When did we become old women?" I said laughing.

"I guess somewhere between two years ago and now."

"Tara, have you told Nia everything about how things went down with Channing? I mean does she know about the abuse, and.... the cheating?"

Tara put her hand on my shoulder, "that is something that I'm not proud of, as you shouldn't be either; but we are working through that, and I am grateful. It's in the past now. It was a mistake, and I'm learning to move past that part of the hurt. As far as the abuse, she knows some things. She knows that it got bad enough that you and Liyah helped me get a restraining order and that led to his arrest. She knows that he'll be in prison in Georgia for another couple of years and that he has no idea where I am. She knows what she needs to know, and God help her, she'd probably try to kill him if she could. She's way too good for me sometimes."

"No, you guys are perfect for one another. I'm just glad you're happy. And I'm glad she knows enough. I didn't ever want to slip and imply something that she wasn't aware of, so I wanted to make sure."

"You're good Chante. She knows pretty much all of my dirty secrets."

I leaned my head on Tara's shoulder and she held my hand. It was so good to have her back in my life.

As much as I didn't want my bachelorette weekend to end, it was pretty nice to get home and see my man and my daughter's face when I walked through the door. Chelsea practically tackled me with the hug she gave me; it was almost like I had been gone for an entire month! When Anthony saw me, I could tell he missed me. He walked up to me and gave me the biggest kiss ever.

"I'm so glad you're back, I missed you," he said.

"Did Chelsea drive you that crazy?"

"No, it wasn't that. I think I just missed you is all. This was the first time we had been separated since I moved here. I guess I was just missing you more than usual."

"Well how was Chelsea? Was she all over the place?"

"Actually no. We had a pretty cool weekend, right Chelsea?" he called out to her.

"Right! It was awesome! We went to the arcade, and the library and the park. Ooo mommy, let me show you the prize he won at the arcade for me!" she said.

"Well, sounds like you guys had a blast," I said as Chelsea dragged me into her room.

After a few minutes, I came back from her room, "she said you are the best stepdad in the world. She wanted to make sure I told you. She is now reading with her headphones on."

"Then my mission was accomplished. Operation Cool Stepdad was a success!" he said.

"Looks like it was," I said laughing. I stepped into the kitchen, washed my hands and proceeded to help Anthony with dinner. He had some low jazz music playing in the background and a glass of wine on the counter.

"I see you are setting a mood around here, huh?"

"I knew you'd be home soon, so I decided to get us some dinner prepared. And I bought your favorite wine."

"Don't you know the way to my heart?"

"Always baby; always."

I gave Anthony a kiss and started setting the table for us. It was truly good to be home, and with each passing day, I knew I was making the best decision by marrying this amazing man.

TWENTY-SEVEN

A few months later....

In the midst of my planning frenzy, I called my mom to get her opinion on floral arrangements for the reception ballroom. I called her on Facetime, just so she could see the mess of flowers that were on the floor of my office.

"Mama, I need your help. Which arrangement looks better?" I said, without any type of greeting or forewarning.

"Well, hey Chante! How are you? I know I taught you manners," she said.

"I'm sorry mama, my head is all over the place these days. Hey! How are you?" I said back with a smirk.

"That's more like it. Now, what is it that you need? Why does your room look like a garden threw up in there?"

"It's because I'm trying to pick out these damn flowers. And you know how much I hate flowers. Tara and Nia said I need to make a decision tonight because I've put it off long enough and they're right. Based on my wedding timeline that Nia helped me with, I should have had decorations finished weeks ago. There was just too much on my mind between planning Anthony's move, finding a bigger place and planning the second wedding of my dreams. I was worn out!

"They look pretty nice Chante, but if you are looking for my opinion, I like the ones on your right; my left."

This is why I loved her, because I loved that one as well, but I needed some confirmation. My mother was always able to give that to me.

"So, now that I have helped you with that traumatic decision, how are other things? How's Anthony? Has he settled in ok?"

"We're doing great actually. He's way more involved with this process than Trey was. He wants to have an opinion on every little thing; even down to the napkins," I said laughing. Truthfully, I enjoyed Anthony being so invested in the process. I don't know why it gave me such a sense of security, but it did.

"Well, just make sure you are sure, baby. I don't mean to...what do you all say... throw shade... anyway, I'm not trying to buy too many 'mother of the bride' dresses, ok? If Anthony is the one, he needs to be the LAST one; ok?"

I rolled my eyes so hard I wish they'd fall out, "yes ma'am. I get it, I messed up my marriage and I am just desensitizing the sanctity and importance of marriage."

"Now Chante quit that! I did not say that. I just said that if he is going to be the one, let him be your one and only. You don't want to be out here like your aunt, married three times going on four; always claiming the new one is 'the one.' Hell if that was the case she should have never divorced the first!"

Now, that made me laugh. My aunt is definitely the female version of a rolling stone. If she didn't feel it anymore for a man, he will definitely know, and she will be packing her bags.

"Don't worry mama, Anthony will be the only one for me forever. He's made me feel...." I sighed, "I have no words. I'm just blown away."

My mother gave me a side eye and gave in, "ok, if you say so. Just make sure you are sure. You don't want to be living in regret; wondering what could have been like...." She stopped. She looked at me as I looked right back at her, quizzically.

"Like who mama?"

"Nobody. I wasn't thinking about anybody." My mother was a terrible liar. I knew she was lying once she opened her mouth to deny what she said. She always looks away and bites her lip.

"Jackie Davis, if you don't tell me what you are talking about, you won't have to worry about your mother of the bride dress; because I will un-invite you."

She rolled her eyes, "fine! I'll give you the tea."

"Mom, you have GOT to stop talking like you're 25."

"Whatever. So, I talk to Trey's mom all the time, right? Well one day she let it slip that he cannot STAND Liyah. Said that she's all bougie and entitled. She never acted that way before, so I don't know what made her change. And she said that Liyah don't even be taking care of TJ; just lets their fancy ass nanny watch him all the time; she probably does that with Chelsea too. Oh, and she said that he misses you and regrets marrying Liyah."

I looked at my mother, stunned. Granted, I could sense some of the bullshit that Trey was going through with Liyah, because of how he interacted with me when he was without her. But to hear my mother say that she knew Trey still missed me definitely threw me for a loop.

"You're lying, ma. I don't believe you. The last thing Trey is thinking about is my cheating ass."

"I'm not lying, Chante. I was talking to his mother and she said those exact words. Trust me, Trey is still in love with you and I think if he could have his way; he'd be running back to you."

"Ma, if that was the case, he wouldn't have hurt me the way he did. Now, I'm not saying I didn't deserve whatever I had coming, because I did cheat. I caused all this mess we're in, but really? Liyah?! Of all women to decide to have a baby with and marry, he chose the person who was supposed to be my sister?! I'm sorry, I can't get close to someone like that. And I'm sure his feelings for me are mutual."

My mother looked at me and rolled her eyes, "If you say so. But trust me Chante, mothers know. And Trey may not be my son-in-law anymore, but I know him. He's miserable, whether you want to believe it or not."

I decided to end the call with my mother with talks of my rehearsal dinner and things like that. Once we were off the phone, my mind was racing. I couldn't believe that she would tell me that! I know she has always been pro-Trey, and ever since Anthony and I became exclusive she has shown a bit of apprehension, almost like she always thought Trey and I would come back together. It was a nice dream to have, but after two years of praying for that and it not happening, I moved on. Sad to say, my mom should too.

TWENTY-EIGHT

In a matter of weeks that seemed to fly by, our rehearsal dinner was upon us. Nia was my right-hand woman this time around and set up a private affair for our closest friends, wedding party and family. Anthony's parents flew in from Chicago and my mother and father came from Atlanta. It was turning out to be a great night.

As Anthony and I boarded our town car to head to the venue, he said, "baby, you look absolutely stunning."

"Thank you. You look amazing as well."

Anthony had on a three-piece all black tux, with a white rose corsage to match mine. His suit was tailored to him perfectly, and he walked with the confidence of a man who just hit the jackpot (I'd like to think that with me, he did). I was wearing a deep purple long-sleeve gown that went all the way down to the floor. I was rocking my new Christian Louboutin pumps that were a Valentine's Day gift from Anthony and wore a white rose corsage on my wrist. My hair was pulled up off my neck, and Anthony kept telling me my smile lit up the entire room.

As we arrived to the banquet room, Nia was standing in front, waiting for our arrival. When she saw us, her mouth dropped.

"Oh my God! You guys look amazing!" she said. She reached over and gave us both a huge hug. I was happy to have Nia here hosting and taking pictures of this moment for me.

"Thank you again, Nia. I can't wait to see what the pictures look like for this. Everything looks perfect," I said.

"Oh girl, don't thank me. I put a team together because there was no WAY I was going to be able to pull this entire thing off on my own," she said laughing.

Nia gestured for us to move further away from her, so she could snap a picture before we walked in. I snuggled up close to Anthony, with my head leaning into his chest. He wrapped his arm around my waist and let his hand rest gently on top of my butt.

"You smell so good, baby. I can't wait to get you home after this. Get my last little piece before I don't get any except on my birthday," he said.

"What are you talking about silly?" I said as I looked up at him.

"You know married couples don't have sex as often as unmarried couples. By this time tomorrow, I will be on a schedule. It'll go from every other night, to every second and fourth Wednesday of the month!"

I let out a loud laugh, "well, they say Wednesday is 'Hump Day', right?" I said.

We both engaged in laughter while Nia took all the candid pictures. When she was finished, she turned towards the room and announced our arrival.

"Attention everyone, I now present to you, the future Mr. and Mrs. Anthony Bishop!"

As we walked in, I could hear all of our friends and family clapping and cheering for us. The embrace was warm and loving and I knew that tonight would be a good night.

The night was filled with dancing and drinking and toasts from all of our family and friends. Everything came together nicely and the food was amazing. Everyone was in their seats, finishing up what was a wonderful meal when Nia told Anthony and I that it was time for our thank you speech.

Anthony got up first, took my hand and escorted me to the stage so that everyone could see us. Nia handed me a mic and as I began to open my mouth, I heard someone say, "Before you say something, I'd like to extend a toast to the happy couple."

I knew that voice; who wouldn't know a voice you've heard your entire life? Just hearing it sent a rage-filled chill up my spine. I wanted to scream, but nothing would come out of my mouth. I looked out into the crowd and made direct eye contact with the person who interrupted me from making my speech.

It was Liyah.

TWENTY-NINE

"What the fuck is she doing here?!" I thought in my head. How the hell did she know this was happening today? I didn't tell anyone. Didn't post it on social media. My family wouldn't even talk to her. I have no clue how she found her way to my rehearsal dinner, but I knew one thing; she wasn't going to ruin it.

Anthony could feel my body get tense and rigid and asked me, "Chante, what is she doing here?"

"I don't know; but she will be leaving very soon."

I walked off the stage and walked towards her. I tried to be as cordial as possible as I walked up to her, but I could already see the whispers of my family members starting. I got so close to Liyah I could have kissed her in the mouth.

"Liyah, I don't know what the fuck is going on, but you need to leave right now. I haven't bothered you or your family, so please do not start shit in here now. We're too old for this shit. How the hell did you even get in here?!"

I looked at her and could tell she was drunk. She was standing in front of me with this tired grin on her face, and I could smell the vodka on her. She never knew how to hold her liquor, but there was a pain lodged deep in her eyes, something had been bothering her; and her drunken stupor led her here.

"I was going to leave you alone, Chante. Let you be happy and move on with your life; but guess what? Since I can't have happiness, your ass can't either."

"What are you talking about, Liyah? What's going on? I

can tell you're drunk. I know we aren't friends anymore, but let me take you in the back and get you some water and we can talk if you like after I give my speech."

"YOU KNOW EXACTLY WHAT YOU DID, CHANTE! AND NOW EVERYONE ELSE IS GOING TO KNOW AS WELL!"

Liyah snatched the mic from me and proceeds to walk away ruin my entire life, "Ladies and gentleman; Anthony, I just want you all to know something about Ms. Chante Thomas, that some of you may not know. Anthony, I know you don't know, and I am so sorry that it had to come to this."

"I'm done with this shit, now. No more game playing," I thought. I began to walk over to Liyah and snatch the damn mic from her, but she turns and I freeze in my tracks. Liyah walks towards me, holding a blade.

"Try and stop me Chante, and I promise I will cut your ass," she said.

"Bitch, have you lost your fuckin' mind?" I was stunned.

Anthony tried to charge at Liyah from behind, and I yell at him, "Baby, stop!"

Liyah swings around and looks at Anthony, "you too, Anthony. You better listen to your girl."

I could hear the gasps in the crowd. My mother was stunned. Anthony's parents ran towards him. I had to be in the Twilight Zone. There was no way this was happening at my rehearsal dinner. Like, who would have thought my ex-best friend would attempt to sabotage my relationship!

I sat there, helpless and defenseless. I knew that Liyah was about to do something stupid and regretful, but there was no stopping her; she was a woman possessed with hurt and revenge. Obviously, she didn't want to ever see me happy; and she was determined to make sure I wasn't.

"So, where do I begin?" Liyah said as she panned the room, "I know some of you are wondering why I'm even here, because of course most of you are family and probably look at me as the home-wreckin' bitch that broke up Trey and Chante. Well, I came here today because that isn't quite how this all played out."

I cringed. I knew this was what she was doing. She came here with the intention of telling everyone, about my past. I looked over at Anthony, and he was fuming. He couldn't believe Liyah was pulling this bullshit, and she was just drunk enough to try and harm someone in the process.

"So, I recently lost my husband. Trey came to me the other day and said that he was still in love with Chante and doesn't want to be with me anymore. He said that he couldn't move on with our life together, knowing that he is secretly pining for someone he once loved more than me; yep, that's exactly how he said it. So naturally, I put the equation together, and realized, that Chante must not have learned her lesson. I can't prove it yet, but I'm sure she's been cheating on you, Anthony. She's been cheating on you because that's her MO. She cheated on Trey with a guy named Roderick, who was so obsessed over her, he killed himself when he couldn't be with her. She even cheated again after that, with one of our closest friend's husbands! Matter of fact, I saw Tara in here and I can't believe she actually forgave you Chante. I would've beat your ass...oh wait, we've already been there. You tried to beat my ass while I was pregnant," she slurred. She then turned back to Anthony, "she's a grimy bitch and she can't be trusted, Anthony. You better run while you still can, because she's cheating on you now. And if not, she will now that Trey is back on the market."

If looks could kill, Liyah would have been dead where she stood. Pissed could not even describe how I felt at that moment. I lashed out at her, "Liyah are you out of your fucking mind?! I am not cheating on Anthony with Trey. Hell, I didn't even know that he wasn't with you!!!"

"Oh, so he didn't tell you how much he missed being with

you, Chante? Huh? He didn't tell you how he wanted you back between conversations about Chelsea?" She put her name in air quotes to imply it was a cover up for more.

I was truly without words, "Liyah, what are you talking about?! I haven't spoken to Trey in months! We haven't exchanged words that had anything to do with anything other than Chelsea. I'm sorry you're going through that with him, and his feelings are his business. I have moved on and I haven't even spoken to Trey!"

"Whatever, Chante! I know what you did. I would have thought that you would have wanted to change the way you were acting, and at least try and learn from your mistakes. But I guess once a cheater, always a cheater."

I was mortified. I tried so many times to stop Liyah from spewing these lies, but she wouldn't listen. I immediately looked at Nia and she had security already walking towards the dance floor to escort Liyah off the premises. My mother was staring at me with tears in her eyes. I whispered to her to call the police so I could file charges for harassment on her. I went and looked for Anthony, I needed to talk to him because this night was just as ruined for him as it was for me.

As everyone was looking around, shocked at what just occurred, I told Nia to make everyone start dancing and drinking, "the entire night is an open bar. My family loves to get drunk and party, they will move past this. I'm going to find Anthony." Nia nodded at me, gave me a big hug and said, "I know you aren't that person anymore Chante. I believe you and only you. Go find your man; you both deserve to be happy."

I walked out of the room and looked for Anthony. He was outside the hotel, staring up into the sky. I could tell he was embarrassed more than any other emotion because I felt the same way.

I walked up to him slowly, "Anthony? Can we talk? I am

so sorry about this."

"Is it true?" he asked me. He never turned around to face me.

I looked at his back, confused, "is what true?"

"Have you been speaking to Trey again?"

"NO! Baby, I haven't talked to Trey. You can check my phone, email, computer, anything. I've had nothing and want nothing to do with him."

"I just need to know if you planned on playing me. Do you even love me? Is this even real? Like...part of me believes you, but the other part of me always knew that I wasn't your first. I wasn't the man who you would always have that connection with. I knew I was fighting some hurt pain and regret. But Chante please tell me you didn't play me like this."

"Anthony, I would never do that," I said as I walked closer to him. I put my hand on his shoulder, "baby, look at me, please."

He turned around and faced me. There were tears in his eyes.

"None of what that crazy bitch said is true."

"So, that means all the other stuff, the cheating, the guy killing himself over you, all that is true?" he asked.

I didn't know what to say, I just begged him to let me explain, "that is not how all of this happened. I need to explain it to you, but tonight is supposed to be about us, not this bullshit!"

"What did you do Chante? I mean, I know what you told me, but between this and all this drama, I don't know if I want to deal with this for the rest of my life. Is this going to be our life together? Always having to play games with your ex and his wife or whoever she is now to him?"

"No! I will do whatever I have to. I will change my number, I will deactivate my personal social media, I will make it so hard for them to talk to me. I don't want anything to do with Trey and Liyah and I wish they would just leave me alone."

"But baby, that's the point. You have a child with this man, and you won't be able to just cut off communication with him for the sake of her. You'll always be tied to him, which means you'll be tied to her."

Anthony walked away from me. I tried to grab his arm, but he snatched away from me and turned around so fast he almost hit me, "Chante, not now. I will see you at home. I need some time right now."

"Anthony, don't do this baby, please."

He walked back over to me, "Chante, I'm fine. I just need a minute. I need to take a breath. I'll be at home. We can talk more later."

He walked off; but then turned back around and kissed me. He kissed me deeply, like he wanted the world to know I belonged to him. I wrapped my arms around him and melted into his arms.

"I did that so you will know that I'm not mad at you. I'm mad at the situation. The drama is just not something I'm used to. This was an embarrassment to the both of us, and best believe, you're going to have to fix this. But I love you with every ounce of my life. You will be my wife, but you have to fix all this extra shit."

I stood there with my face in my hands, not even knowing where to start. I knew all of this was going to come to a head, but I didn't know it would happen like this. I could hear Nia behind me, telling everyone that we appreciated everyone's attendance, but it was probably best that the party get cut short. I could feel people filing around me, walking out of the door. I could hear the whispers of some of our guests wondering what Liyah was talking about, some accused her of being drunk, others hugged me and told me it would be alright. Anthony's parents walked past me like I was a ghost. My parents hugged me. My mother held me until everyone cleared out and asked me if I was ok. I told her I was, and that I would try to handle everything.

I just wanted to go back to my apartment and never be seen again. Liyah had embarrassed me completely in front of my family, in front of Chelsea, in front of everyone I considered a close friend. She would never be forgiven for this. If her goal was to make me miserable, then congratulations, I am officially miserable.

THIRTY

I turned the key on my apartment door and walked in. My mother was in town for the weekend, and we both felt it would be a good idea that Chelsea stay with her while I talked to Anthony. The entire apartment was dark, so I called out for Anthony.

"Ant? Baby?"

"Yea."

"Thank God. He's at least here," I thought.

I walked back to my bedroom and saw him on my bed, watching the highlights from the game. He wouldn't look at me. I walked in front of my TV and looked at him. My face was puffy, and my eyes were swollen from crying all the way home.

"I'm not with Trey, Anthony. That bitch is lying. She wants to ruin my life, as if she hasn't already gotten what she wanted from me, she has to take more from me." I walked over to him and bent down low enough so that we were eye to eye. I put my hand on his cheek and forced him to look me in my eyes, "I swear Anthony, you can look in my phone, check every ounce of this apartment. Do whatever you need to do but I am not lying. I am not, nor do I have the desire to even be with Trey."

"I believe you, Chante."

I sighed with relief, "good. I don't know what is going on with her, but I will get to the bottom of that shit."

"I'm just embarrassed, babe. We were doing good, our lives were fine, and now I have to wonder if we are going to be dealing with this drama for the rest of our lives. It's just not what I signed up for."

"It's not what I want either. You have no idea what I've been dealing with Liyah. Ever since she married Trey, she's made it a point to be shady and petty, and just recently she accused me of sneaking around with Trey! I told her that was bullshit. I knew something was wrong with her then, but I told her to leave me alone and I told Trey to tell her as well and I hadn't heard anything about it since."

"Why didn't you tell me?"

"Do you want me to be honest? I thought it was stupid bullshit and I didn't want to bother you with it. It was before she had sent you the stupid message, so you found out about it anyway."

"Oh"

"If I knew I was dealing with drama, I would have never allowed you to get so close to me; seriously. There was no point in putting anyone in my life if my life was messy, and I love you too much to involve you in any of that. I want you; and I want an easy life. I don't want to have to deal with this, but I will handle it in the morning."

"Well you can't handle it in the morning, because you have an important appointment."

I looked at him and smiled faintly, "you're right. I'm marrying the love of my life tomorrow. Nothing is going to stop me from doing that."

Anthony buried his head into my chest and let out a deep sigh. We both felt the same way; this day was emotionally draining. We had gone through our first battle together, and definitely had some wounds; but we seemed to come out surviving. Anthony turned off the TV, undressed and got into bed. I went to the bathroom, removed my makeup, threw on his t-shirt and climbed into bed with him. I laid my head on his chest and he held me all night. I was asleep in minutes.

The next morning, I woke up and Anthony wasn't there. I freaked out and shot up out of the bed around 5am, wondering where he went. When I looked around the room, I saw my phone was lit up with a message. It was from Anthony.

"I forgot, the groom shouldn't see the bride before the wedding, so I came to stay with my brother in his room. I'll see you at the altar beautiful. I love you, Ant."

I wrote him back a message:

"I thought you left me. I'll see you later Mr. Bishop."

"Never, Mrs. Bishop."

THIRTY-ONE

The Wedding Day...

When I walked in, Tara, Nia and my mother all looked at me. Chelsea was right underneath my mom, smiling at me. Her hair and small touches of lip gloss and blush were already in place.

Nia broke the awkward silence in the room, "well, you look like shit. And not the 'my man rocked my world before marriage' shit."

"Nia! Really? In front of my mother?!" I said.

"Oh girl, hush! I was young once. I wish I had a man to rock my world every night."

I made sure to tell my mother to never repeat those words to me again, as we all laughed and gave each other hugs.

"Are you ok sweetie?" Tara asked.

"I'm fine. Anthony and I are fine. He is at least here because I saw his car in the parking lot. We are good." I said.

"In that case, let me get my team in position and you need your hair and makeup done because you aren't going to mess up my good shots with these puffy eyes," Nia said.

I agreed and all three of us began to get ready. My mother and Chelsea went and walked around the church for a while and also went to check on Anthony.

I went into the private bathroom and sat down. I took a deep breath and took the moment to take in the celebration of me finding new love. I never thought it would happen, but it has. I made sure Liyah and Trey were the furthest things from my mind today, because it was all about me and Anthony. I took out my dress and began to start the process of going from regular Chante Thomas, to the future Chante Thomas-Bishop.

"You are gorgeous. I am speechless," Tara said as she touched up my makeup. Nia was moving around the both of us, snapping pictures before the ceremony.

"Nia, you are not supposed to be working today. Why do you even have your camera?" I asked.

"I couldn't stand to let this moment pass without you being photographed. Trust me, when I touch it up, you will thank me for capturing the moment." She said.

She knew that would shut me up. I was on cloud nine at this point. I was finally to the day that I would be marrying my soulmate. I couldn't believe that we made it here especially after last night's drama, but he never lost hope or faith in me and knew I was more than my past. He took a chance on me, and now I am marrying that beautiful man.

Tara was in charge of doing my makeup and she was doing an amazing job. She was putting on her final touches when my mother walked into the room.

"Ok ladies, time to take your places. It is almost showtime!"

I looked back at my mother, "mama, how do I look?"

My mother stood there, mouth agape, "Baby.... you look so beautiful baby."

I smiled at her approval.

"Are you happy?" she said.

"What do you mean?"

"I'm going to ask you this one last time about Anthony just to be sure. Are you happy?"

"Happier than I've been in a long time, ma."

"In that case, I love him and always will."

A few minutes later, my mother and I broke our trance and prepared to have them take their places in preparation for me to walk down the aisle. Everyone gave me a small kiss on the cheek, and left the room as I took a few minutes to myself. I looked in the mirror, examining my dress, admiring at how perfect it fit me. I ran my hands against the jewels that were on my dress, admiring how beautiful I was when I heard a voice; a distinct, yet surprising voice. It was one that I didn't think I would hear at my wedding, yet here it was clear as day and filled my mind with immediate regret.

"Chante...?"

THIRTY-TWO

I couldn't believe the voice I had just heard. I turned around to find Trey standing in the doorway to my room, a bouquet of flowers in his hands.

"Hello, Chante."

"Trey? What are you doing back here? How did you even get back here?"

"Can I get a minute of your time? Just one minute please."

"Trey I can't do this with you right now. What the hell are you doing here? It's my wedding! Is Liyah with you because I've already taken measures to put a restraining order on that bitch. I don't even want you here."

"No! No! She's not with me. Matter of fact, she won't be with me for a while."

"What?"

"I left her Chante. I couldn't do it anymore. All the pressure, the drama, the constant jealousy. I couldn't love her like she wanted me to; I couldn't love her like I love you."

I thought I was having a heart attack. My heart was pounding, and I could hear a ringing in my ears. I thought my hearing was playing tricks on me, so I asked again, "you what?!"

"I said it, Chante. I love you. I still love you and I told Liyah this. She told me what she did yesterday too, and I'm so sorry. You know I would never want something to get in the way of your happiness."

I was stunned, "yet, here you are, attempting to get in the way of my happiness and convince yourself that this is supposed to make me love you. Where the hell is this even coming from? I can't do this with you right now. I'm walking down the aisle in fifteen minutes!"

"I know, and I'll be quick. You were right, Chante. Liyah was nothing more than a rebound. I rebounded hard when she was there for me. But now that we're together, all she seems to care about is one-upping you. She always wants to have the upper hand in everything. She's controlling as hell, she doesn't even take care of TJ that much; she is everything I never wanted in a woman, and I wasted my marriage on her. I should have worked it out with you. I should have always chosen you, Chante."

"Trey, I don't know where this is coming from, but this conversation is over. I want you to leave."

"Wait! I know what I did was wrong, and I can never forgive myself for it. Choosing Liyah should have never been an option. I'm sorry for that. I'm sorry for betraying you and causing Liyah to betray your friendship. I went to her out of spite; I wanted you to hurt just like you hurt me. If I knew she would be this way.... I.... I don't know. I just know it was wrong."

I didn't know what to say. It's been four years since Trey and I divorced. Four years. The first two years I prayed and prayed for him to take me back. I wanted to be forgiven and he would not give me the time of day. Now, as I am entering my second chance at happiness, he is pulling this bullshit?

"Trey, I appreciate the things you have said, and I accept your apologies. But you have to know that I do not love you that way anymore. You were my first love; my first husband and the father of my beautiful daughter. You will always have a place in my heart because we were also good friends as well as lovers. But now, I am in love again. Someone found me and saw past my horrible flaws and decided I was still worth loving. Trey I tried to get you to see that in me, but you didn't want to try again. Why now? Why are you crawling back begging for my love on the day I am marrying another man?"

"Because I know that deep down, you still love me too. You still miss what we had, and we can both just run away and be together."

"Are you serious right now? Is this a joke? Does Liyah know you're here Trey, because I don't need any more drama like I had at my rehearsal dinner. She already thinks you're cheating on her with me and I don't need that shit right now," I said to him.

"Liyah doesn't know I'm here. But I don't care about Liyah right now, Chante. I realized that I have to get this off my chest. I didn't realize how much I missed you until I realized that you were about to start a new life with a new man."

"Trey, look. I told myself that I would never betray another man and ruin my life the way I did. I hate that we had to experience that together; and I'd be lying if I said I had no love in my heart for you. You were my first everything and the father to my first child. You will always have a place in my heart, but I can't sit here and say I'm willing to throw away what I have with Anthony to go back to you. You made your choice to be with Liyah and establish a life with her. I don't feel that way for you anymore. I'm marrying Anthony now; we've both moved on now, so that's just where we are now."

I stood up and walked past Trey as he stood in my doorway, "you may want to go out the back, I don't need anyone to see you back here."

The flowers were hanging lifelessly from his hand by his side. His face wore defeat. I could tell that being with Liyah stressed him. The stress lines were apparent. I hated that Liyah had worn him down to nothing with her drama and bullshit, but that was no longer my problem or my fight. I had found love when I never thought I would again. I'll be damn if I lose it a second time.

I walked away from Trey and I didn't look back until I heard him walk off. He was going in the opposite direction, towards the side exit of the church. I was praying no one saw him coming in or leaving.

As I walked through the foyer of the church, I could feel the butterflies in my stomach. I began to flashback to the day I married Trey. I was so much younger, and it was so long ago. I was a different woman then. I knew so much more now than I knew then and I was more prepared now than I was before. When I watched the ushers pull the doors of the church open, I watched a flood of people in the church pews stand to watch me walk down the aisle. My father awaited me at the start of the aisle and grabbed my arm. He kissed me lightly on the cheek and proceeded to escort me down. I looked up and saw Anthony. That is when our eyes met. At that moment, everyone and everything else didn't matter.

It didn't matter what happened the night before. It didn't matter that Trey tried to profess his love to me moments before; nothing else mattered. I locked eyes with Anthony, and tears streamed down my face. My heart was filled with so much joy in that moment, and I was overjoyed to know that I would be with him for the rest of my life.

We made it down the aisle and I was finally face to face with the love of my life. Nia was in the front, capturing every moment for me. When the pastor asked who was giving me away, my father gleamed with pride and said, "I am. Her mother and I." I looked back towards my mother and mouthed, *"I love you."* She blew a kiss.

I turned and faced Anthony in this moment. His eyes were glossy, which let me know he had shed some tears as well. I held my hands in his, and I could feel his shaking slightly. He was so nervous.

"It's ok. It's just you and me," I said to him in a whisper.

He nodded.

I smiled at him. Assured him he was ok.

The ceremony began, and the pastor spoke. The entire time, Anthony wouldn't let go of my hands. And I wouldn't let go of his. Our calm was found within each other.

When it was time to exchange vows, Anthony and I agreed to write our own. Anthony went first.

"I hope I can get through this without messing up. I tried to memorize the whole thing," there were small chuckles in the crowd of family and friends.

"Chante, from the moment I met you, I knew God sent you to me. I never told you this, but I was at a point in my life where I didn't think true love was possible for me. After my last relationship, I didn't think I was worthy of having love, and I thought maybe I didn't know how to love properly. But then God sent you to me, and I knew that you were the only woman I wanted to be with for the rest of my life. I knew that if you let me, I would be the best man I could be for you. I wouldn't be perfect, and I wouldn't strive for perfection because no man is perfect; but I would respect you and Chelsea. I would love you and Chelsea, and I would honor you and Chelsea. You have become my number 1 priorities, and I promise that I will live the rest of my days loving, honoring and cherishing you, Chante; if you will let me."

There was a chorus of sniffles, tears and 'awwws' echoing across the church. I was stunned at the words Anthony said. He always joked about how he was not the writing type, and how he always 'left the creative writing thing up to me', but said that he would keep the vows a surprise because he wanted to put his best foot forward and show me his best effort. And boy did he blow it out of the water.

"Well, for someone who's not a writer, you sure did pretty good, Anthony," I said. There was some laughter across the room.

Next, it was my turn. I took a deep breath. The butterflies started to flutter again, but I tried to keep them under control at least for another few minutes to get through the vows.

I took a deep sigh, "ok. So, this wasn't supposed to happen. Love wasn't supposed to happen twice for me. I took advantage the first time, so I wasn't supposed to be lucky. And then you came along. You loved me despite my past, despite my scars and despite the pain I may have caused. You took on the challenge of loving me when I was even too broken to love myself. I promise to love you, and I will always promise to love you. I will give my all to you and to this marriage and that you will never have to worry about. I appreciate you, and I honor you. You have come in and stepped up and been the man I needed so desperately. I have fallen madly in love with you, and I promise to keep being in love with you forever."

Anthony took his hand and caressed my cheek, wiping the tears as they fell down my face. He smiled at me, "that was beautiful babe. I love you too."

The rings were exchanged, and the ceremony was finalized. I was officially Mrs. Chante Thomas-Bishop. I had not felt this much joy in my heart in a long time, and I was so blessed that it was with Anthony. During our reception, we walked around to all of our family and friends and thanked them for coming. Several of them had questions about the antics of last night, but I just told them that it was nothing for them to be concerned with, because clearly Anthony and I had moved on.

Anthony and I danced and danced the night away in each other's arms. He didn't leave my side at the reception and I never wanted him to. We were glad to have finally turned the page into our new chapter of life together.

So, it's like I said, happily ever after happened twice in one lifetime. After our wedding, Anthony and I spent a week in Turks and Caicos for our honeymoon. We had an amazing time. We left our cell phones in DC, so it was just us and time. I did bring my work cell with me, but it was only to call Chelsea and Nia while she and Tara watched her. Tara now had Josh with her, so it was nice to see the two reconnect after so long.

I found out shortly after I got back from my honeymoon that Trey had moved away from Miami and closed down his restaurant there. No one; not even his mother knew where he went. I was a little upset with him, because I knew after a while, Chelsea would ask questions about where he went, and it wasn't fair to her to disappear on her like that. I hoped he would at least tell his mother something so she could let me know for the sake of Chelsea. TJ stayed with Liyah when they left, and Liyah went back to Atlanta to stay with her parents, and eventually she and Trey started the process for a divorce. It was clear that there were some insecurity issues there. Liyah went to a treatment center to receive counseling and help for the issues she was having after losing Trey, and also her outburst with me. Turns out, the drinking was a lot worse than what I ever would have imagined. But I was glad she was getting the help she needed.

As for me and Anthony, we were happy just where we were. We were working on finding a new house to buy and living our best lives. Life couldn't have come around to a fuller circle for me, and I know that I learned my lesson from the first go round. If I'm having issues in my marriage, I will never play with fire again.

SIX MONTHS LATER...

I woke up to the most wonderful smell ever. I immediately realized that it was Saturday morning, Anthony's favorite morning to cook. I smiled and got up out of bed and prepared to go see my man in the kitchen cooking up a special breakfast for us.

Chelsea was with Trey and his mother for summer break, and during that time, Anthony usually takes about a week off so that we will have our own little vacation as well. Anthony and I were enjoying our time staying up late and sleeping in and having days of doing absolutely nothing. Last night was no different, as I woke up from a coma after a night of our version of "Netflix and chill."

I throw on his t-shirt and walked down the hall to the kitchen and I could start to hear the music get louder and louder. He loved playing R&B on the mornings that he cooked breakfast. As he saw me emerge from the bedroom he looked up and smiled, "Good morning, beautiful." He walked over to me, placed his hand on my stomach and said, "hello to you too, beautiful."

Anthony and I had found out I was pregnant about six weeks ago, and we couldn't have been more excited. He had always wanted children and we wasted no time getting down to business after we walked down that aisle.

"Good morning baby. What's on the menu for today?"

"French toast, bacon, eggs, hash browns and your personal favorite; mimosas." He said with a grin on his face.

"I walked over to him, stole a piece of French toast and kissed him on the cheek, "you treat me so well, boo." I said.

I sat down in the living room and flipped through my magazine, periodically looking over it to admire him in the kitchen. I couldn't help but relish in the fact that life was truly getting better for me. I had a man in my life that I loved unconditionally, that loved me for my flaws and amazing qualities as well. He looked back over at me and smiled, "what are you staring at over there, Mrs. Bishop?"

"Nothing. Just admiring how good you look, and how lucky I am." I said.

"I'm sure not as lucky as I am."

Anthony walked over to me and kissed me. "Breakfast is served, my love."

I got up and prepared to walk over to the dining room table, when I heard a knock at the door. Anthony was in the kitchen preparing our plates, so I told him, "I'll get it babe."

I looked out of the peephole and did not see anyone. When I opened the door, I saw a dozen red roses on my doorstep. I looked over my shoulder and asked Anthony, "Are you playing games with me, boy?"

"What do you mean?" he said.

"Did you have these delivered to the house?"

"No. If I wanted to give you flowers, I would have had them sitting on the table when you came out of the bedroom for breakfast."

"Well then, is someone sending YOU flowers?"

"If they are, I definitely didn't ask for them," he laughed. "Just look and see if there is a card on them that will tell you if there is some chick sending me flowers."

I picked up the bouquet and walked back into the house.

There was a small white card sticking out of the beautiful array of flowers, so I picked it out and opened it. When I saw it, my body froze. I didn't even realize that I dropped the flowers until Anthony swung his head around and rushed over to me.

"Baby, what's the matter? Who are the flowers from?" he said.

I didn't respond. All I said was, "I need to call Tara."

I ran down to my bedroom and snatched my phone off the phone charger. I speed dialed Tara's number immediately. She answered on the first ring.

"Tara? I need to ask you something. Did you get a package this morning; a bouquet of flowers?"

"I know, Chante. I got mine yesterday," was all she said. I could hear that she was just as shook as I was.

"I can't believe this, Tara. How the fuck did this happen?!"

"I don't know. But I know we need to figure something out quick. Looks like we don't have much time."

I hung up the phone and tried to catch my breath. All this time, I was doing fine. I didn't know how Tara was doing regarding the situation, but I'm sure neither one of us had a reason to believe that something like this would happen. I looked down at the card, and tears began to flow from my eyes.

The card was very simple, but it rocked my entire world.

"Hey sweetie, I'll be seeing you very soon. Hope you waited for me."

-C.M.

Anthony walked up behind me and asked "Baby, who are the flowers from? And why are you crying?"

"Remember when I told you about the guy who was emotionally abusive to me and physically abusive to Tara?"

"Yes. I remember," He said.

"He's getting out of prison," I said. "I don't know when, but he said he will see me soon."

I was sick to my stomach. I ran to my room and shut the door. I could hear Anthony at the door; I could feel his presence, but he wouldn't knock. He knew I needed a minute, but he didn't want to leave me alone.

I couldn't believe that after all this time, my past would come rushing back into my life like this. I knew Anthony wouldn't let anything happen to me, but my concern was more for Tara than anyone else. I told Anthony I needed a minute then I would be out to eat breakfast. When he walked away from the door, I sent Tara a text:

Tara, what are we going to do? How did he find us? I don't want this fool to hurt me or you and Josh. If you need me, Anthony and I are here.

Just as we were living our lives as normally as we could, one bouquet of roses was enough to shatter all of that to pieces. Channing had shown his true colors; and even if Tara wasn't, I was concerned about what he would or could be capable of. Within minutes my phone buzzed with a text back from her.

He won't ruin our lives again.

We will talk soon.

ACKNOWLEDGEMENTS

I didn't know what "labor of love" felt like until I started writing this book. It's my most emotional work yet, because it was birthed out of a true mental and emotional struggle.

Playing with Fire II took a lot longer than it needed to, to be written. It was at no one else's fault but my own, but there was so much happening with myself that I couldn't see past the fog.

There were days I hated writing. Days I hated myself and didn't feel I was good enough to be a writer. Days where I wanted to throw my whole draft in the recycle bin and never write. Maybe there will never be a continued story of Chante and Trey's life. Who wants to really know anyway?

I didn't think anyone cared whether I wrote another word or not; and I lost the love I had for writing so much I didn't care. The days and weeks that writers block would hit me we're unbearable. Paired with the excruciating guilt of not being able to give yourself and others what they wanted, hurt me.

There were a lot of highs and lows in between the journey of writing PWFII, and if it wasn't for me finding the love I have for myself, and the love I have for this ability to create art, I wouldn't be here today; at the end of my journey, finishing the long-awaited sequel to Playing with Fire.

I wanted to continue the story of Chante and show the world, that there is redemption at the end of betrayal. There is a world where you can be forgiven, and you can be loved again even if you were the one who caused the pain. Chante was not your typical character; she was the one who caused the pain; she cast the first stone, and yet she was still able to find the love she needed. She was able to also have a happy ending, and the karma was life was not all it seemed to be for Trey in the end.

I am typically not one to single anyone out, because I would feel guilty if I left someone out. So, I will say this, you know who you are when I say these words, and if they affect you, then you know you are someone who I am talking to:

Thank you for being in my corner, for supporting me, pushing me, encouraging me, asking about my process, asking about my progress, making me write, telling me to stop procrastinating. Thank you for telling me that you wanted to read more, that you needed to know what happened next. Thank you for telling me what I needed to hear in order to be better at my writing. Thank you for giving me the tools I needed to improve with each word I've written. I hope I have made you proud this time around.

Love you all, and enjoy,

Whit C.

About the Author

Whitney Cason is a young and vibrant writer of poetry, novels and short stories. She published her first novel in 2016, titled *Playing with Fire*. She also published her first poetry collection, *From a Lover's Mouth*. In 2019, she published a second novel, a continuation of the Playing with Fire series, titled *How it Really Went Down*, and her second collection of poetry, *A Soul's Journey*. This is the third installment and the official sequel of the *Playing with Fire* series.

Whitney currently lives in Greensboro, North Carolina. with her daughter, Kynnedy.

When she is not writing, Whitney enjoys reading, listening to music, and spending quality time with family and friends.

www.ingramcontent.com/pod-product-compliance
Lightning Source LLC
Chambersburg PA
CBHW060316260626
47160CB00007B/2639

* 9 7 8 0 9 9 9 9 1 0 6 0 3 7 *